MISTLETOE MOTHER

BY
JOSIE METCALFE

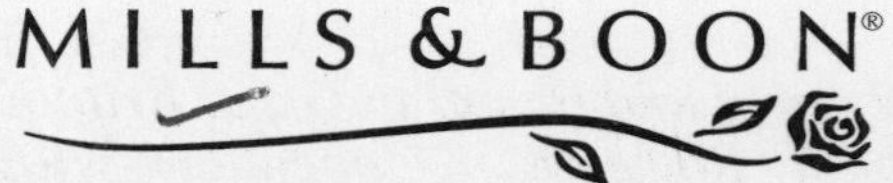

First published in Great Britain 2001
Large Print edition 2002
Harlequin Mills & Boon Limited,
Eton House, 18-24 Paradise Road,
Richmond, Surrey TW9 1SR

ISBN 0 263 17177 9

Set in Times Roman 16½ on 18 pt.
17-0602-51680

Printed and bound in Great Britain
by Antony Rowe Ltd, Chippenham, Wiltshire

CHAPTER ONE

'WHAT on *earth* am I doing in Scotland in the middle of winter?' Seth Gifford groaned in disgust.

The snow seemed to be coming at him from every direction at once, and as fast as it was chilling his face and piling up on his hair and coat, it was also melting down the back of his neck in freezing trickles.

He could barely see the outline of the tiny cottage through the wildly whirling flakes surrounding him, even though it was just a few paces away. The path was slippery, too, especially with a cumbersome box of groceries in his arms.

'Whose stupid idea was this, anyway?' he grumbled aloud, knowing that there was no one in this whirling white wilderness to hear him. For the first time in his life he was completely alone, with not a single person for miles around him. Even his unofficial chauffeur was too far away by now to hear him talking to himself, on his way back to the cosy warmth of his cottage in the village at the other end of the glen. It would be two weeks, when Christmas and the New Year's celebrations were all over, before the elderly man would retrieve him from his solitude in this tiny croft.

Solitude, he repeated as he made a second journey between the pile of boxes the elderly man had helped to offload at the gate and the tiny porch sheltering the front door. Well, it was another less emotive word for loneliness, he supposed. But, then, he seemed to have been lonely for so much of his life that another two weeks wouldn't make much difference.

His colleagues back at the hospital had been looking forward to the coming festive season with their usual mix of anticipation and resignation, depending on their family situations and whether they were rostered on or off duty.

He'd barely registered feelings either way. Since Fran had died he'd had no really close friends. There was only his brother left to share the holiday season with, and he'd had his own agenda for years. Not even the matchmaking efforts of the boldest of his co-workers had been able to persuade him into starting a new relationship, and he certainly wasn't into brief flings.

There had only ever been three women in his life who had mattered to him. First, Margaret, the mother who had died so tragically when he was only sixteen, then Fran, the wife whose disregard for hospital rules and regulations had exacted such a terrible price. The third had been a colleague in his own Obs and Gyn department who he'd foolishly believed would be there for him when he needed her most.

Instead, she had disappeared from his life without a trace and he tried to avoid even thinking about her, let alone saying her name.

'So much for third time lucky,' he muttered grimly as he searched in one pocket after another to find the elusive key while bracing the last box against the frame of the door. With a growl of frustration he dragged first one glove and then the other off with his teeth, beyond caring when only one of them managed to drop *inside* the box. The other disappeared towards his feet, probably destined to be whirled away and buried under a mountain of snow.

He supposed it was his own fault that he'd ended up here, bearing in mind his increasingly sombre moods over the last year or so. The fact that he'd never been able to confide in any of his colleagues had only added to the stress. Sometimes it had felt as if the only thing that had kept him sane had been the fact that he'd had patients depending on his skills to bring their babies safely into the world, but even so…

Really, he admitted silently, remembering the pointed comments he'd had from more than one of those colleagues, it was probably just sheer luck on his part that his whole team hadn't ganged up to banish him to the North Pole.

'On second thoughts, perhaps they have,' he muttered in disgust as the rising wind blew a veritable blizzard of snowflakes around him in spite of the partial protection of the porch. But he hadn't been *that* bad, had he, that they'd want to dump him in the middle of this? At Christmas, too…?

He threw a quick glance over his shoulder and grimaced. The brief glimpse he'd had of starkly beautiful winter mountains had disappeared almost as quickly as his unofficial taxi. The snow was falling faster now and the last of the daylight was almost gone. If this kept up he was going to be completely stranded in a matter of hours and who knew how long it would be before the roads would be clear again? If he didn't find the key soon, perhaps they'd find his body still frozen on the doorstep when the snows finally thawed in the spring…

'Gotcha!' He finally closed his chilly fingers around the elusive key and dragged it out of his pocket. 'Now all I've got to do is get the wretched thing to fit into the lock.'

With a grunt of satisfaction he heard the snick as the key turned but when he leant against the door it remained stubbornly closed, almost as though it were still firmly locked.

'That's all I need!' he groaned in disbelief. 'Am I going to have to break in to get out of the cold?' It certainly wouldn't be very cosy inside if he had to spend the next two weeks combating a howling gale coming in through a broken window.

'The key *must* fit, otherwise what was the point in giving it to me?'

The envelope bearing the key and the address of this little cottage had been hand-delivered to his office just two days ago. He hadn't recognised the handwriting and no one would admit responsibility, but everyone he'd asked had been almost insultingly eager that he should take the suggested holiday.

Another flurry of snow sifted its way down the back of his neck and for just a second he contemplated finding his mobile phone to ask for his unofficial taxi driver to come straight back to collect him. Then the thought of dragging a man almost old enough to be his grandfather out again on a night like this resurrected a little of his pride.

'You're not caving in at the first hurdle,' he told himself fiercely. 'The others might have been half joking when they sent you here, but you're the only one who *really* knows how much you need to get your head together. Now, *think*, man. Why didn't the key work?

Perhaps the door's warped, or something. Small wonder if this weather is par for the time of year.'

As he bent down to deposit his ungainly burden before trying again, he suddenly realised that he was still talking to himself and grimaced. Was this a new habit? Surely the isolation wasn't getting to him already.

As he straightened up to try the key again, the increasingly vicious wind caught the end of his scarf and flipped it right across his face just as the door swung silently open in front of him. He blinked as light and warmth spilled over him like some unearthly benediction and suddenly realised that he had an unexpected welcoming committee.

'How far have you got, then?'

Ella bent awkwardly towards the hearth to lift the corner of the tea towel and peered at the rising dough underneath it with a satisfied smile.

The bread wouldn't be ready to go into the oven for another twenty minutes or so. Just enough time to get the fire going so that the oven would be hot enough to make a crusty top on each loaf. 'Just the way you taught me, Granny,' she murmured as she set the timer, feeling as ever that her grandmother's spirit would never really leave the cottage she'd loved so much. 'Put the bread in first, when the oven's hottest, then pastry, then cakes as the temperature slowly falls.'

Later, she would be putting in a casserole to simmer slowly overnight, but her supper to-night was going to be at least one steaming bowl of home-made leek and potato soup with a couple of slices of hot, freshly baked bread. 'If I can get the fire hot enough, that is,' she grumbled as she lowered herself heavily to her knees and reached for a handful of kindling. 'I'm moving even slower than Granny did, and she was eighty years old and riddled with ar-thritis.'

After the last seven or eight months, the whole baking process was almost second na-ture now—lighting a fire in the old-fashioned cloam oven from the briskly burning embers of the open hearth, then raking out the fire when the oven reached the right temperature to bake the bread.

Her father had wanted to replace the centuries-old hearth with a modern cooker to make his mother's life a little easier but she'd stubbornly clung to the methods she'd grown up with. In spite of the effort involved, Ella could understand the attraction of the old ways, especially on such a cold day.

The fire was blazing brightly in the depths when she shut the oven door and sat back on her heels, glad that her grandmother had resisted. It might be old-fashioned, but the wide fireplace with the cloam oven built into the wall of one side of it was certainly the most appropriate for this sort of weather.

'Not only does it keep me warm but I can use it for cooking my food, too, and all without worrying about power cuts or running out of gas bottles.'

The swiftly running stream that hurried past the back of the cottage provided her water, via the totally modern tanks and pipes at one end of the tiny loft. Granny had been easily persuaded that there was no good reason to carry buckets of water or make trips to the 'privy' when she could have the labour-saving convenience of running water and an inside bathroom.

At the same time, the force of the stream on its downward rush had been unobtrusively utilised to provide all the power she needed for lighting and a fridge. In a really bitter winter the volume of water might be diminished by ice, but so far the little diesel generator hidden away in one of the outhouses as an emergency backup hadn't been needed at all.

Anyway, she preferred the oil lamps her grandmother had once relied on, and she had a plentiful supply of candles. There was plenty of wood split for burning, with several days' worth neatly piled beside the fire and even a stack of peat if she got desperate.

Real pioneer stuff, as her sister Sophia was prone to tease, her pretty face screwed up in an expression of mock disgust as she examined her neatly manicured nails.

And it was just teasing, Ella knew with a renewed surge of gratitude for Sophia's generosity. They'd both loved their visits to the little cottage and had revelled in the freedom to roam far and wide no matter what time of year they'd come. It seemed almost impossible that they would never again hear the soft burr of Granny's voice as she bade them come in for their tea, or the stories she would tell of the creatures that shared the glen with her.

It had been her bequest to the two of them that they should share the cottage between them and it had been Sophia's idea that Ella should stay here until she decided what direction her life was going to take.

She'd originally offered to sell the cottage so that Ella could use the money to live on, only admitting how much she'd hated the thought of losing it when Ella had turned the idea down without a second thought.

Staying here had been the best solution all round. She had chickens for eggs and she'd become almost self-sufficient once she'd got the vegetable garden going. As for the rest, it hadn't taken long to dust off her grandmother's spinning wheel so that she had goods to sell or barter in the way of isolated rural communities for the other things she needed.

Her thoughts were wandering happily over the little successes that had helped to bring her out of the depression that had driven her here when a sound outside the front of the cottage drew her attention.

A car? She began the struggle to get to her feet. 'If that's Malcolm coming to check up on me again I shall give him a piece of my mind. I told him I had plenty of everything and he shouldn't be driving around when the weather's like this. Doesn't he realise that Morag worries about him?'

She used the arm of the chair to heave herself upright and stood puffing for a moment while she listened to the sound of thuds and bumps in the little porch. She hardly needed more food and she had enough wood stacked within easy reach to last for a couple of months at least. She even had a source of fresh milk, delivered daily to the end of the track by one of the MacLain lads on his way into the village. Anything else she needed, including help, she just had to lift the phone to find any number of people willing to offer, such was her grandmother's legacy within the tiny community.

The only thing she hadn't got—and that Malcolm couldn't deliver—was some extra energy.

'Oh, I'll be so glad when I've lost some of this weight,' she grumbled as she waddled towards the door. 'The next three weeks can't go fast enough. I can't wait to see my feet again—no offence, baby!' she added as she slid a hand under the voluminous hand-knitted jumper which had once been her father's and patted the taut mound of her belly.

For a moment it almost sounded as if someone was trying to use a key in the lock, but before she could think anything of it she was distracted by a hefty kick against her hand.

'So, you want to get out, do you? If you take my advice, you'll wait until the weather's a bit better, or at least until daylight,' she murmured fondly as she reached out to slide the old-fashioned bolt aside, her other hand reaching for the light switch that was almost never used. 'We don't want to make Malcolm do too many trips in the snow.'

She pulled the door open and was momentarily blinded by a flurry of whirling snowflakes before she realised that, whoever he was, the man on her doorstep wasn't sixty-four-year-old Malcolm.

For just a moment the reflexes she'd honed when she'd lived in the city nearly had her slamming the door in the stranger's face. Then common sense stayed her hand.

Whoever he was, and whatever had brought him to her door, he needed help to find his way back to the road, although how he could possibly have mistaken her little track for the properly surfaced glen road she had no idea.

'Are you lost?' she asked, and had to suppress a smile when she heard echoes of her grandmother's accent in her voice. When she'd lived in the city all those years, during her training, her own accent had almost disappeared. Until this moment she hadn't realised that it had returned stronger than ever.

She shivered as the wind forced its way through the narrow gap between door and jamb, glad of her thick jumper and the fact that she wasn't out in that awful weather.

As her visitor fought to subdue the ends of his scarf the light over his head suddenly illuminated a head of thick dark hair, tousled by the wind in spite of the neatness of the style and dotted with glittering shards of ice. He blinked to rid sinfully long lashes of the latest sprinkling of snowflakes and revealed eyes the colour of burnished steel.

'If this isn't Buchanan's Croft, I *am* lost,' her visitor said wryly.

Every hair went up on the back of Ella's neck when she heard that all-too-familiar voice and she had an awful sinking feeling inside her that wasn't helped by the vigorous football match being enacted inside her.

'And why would you be looking for the Buchanan's Croft?' she asked, copying his 'foreign' pronunciation of the name as she had to raise her voice over the rising sound of the wind. She had a dreadful feeling as the scene played out in front of her eyes that her peaceful existence was just about to shatter beyond repair. This was all of her worst nightmares come to life and she would far rather have shouted at him to go away than hold a polite conversation on her doorstep.

'Because I'm supposed to be staying at the croft for the next two weeks and I seem to have been delivered to the wrong place.' He was searching his pockets as though trying to find something. 'Is it far away?'

'Staying?' she squeaked as the situation just got worse and worse. 'But…'

'Ah! Here it is!' he exclaimed as he pulled a crumpled sheet of paper out of an inside pocket. 'There's the address, right there.'

He held the pale blue slip towards her and she leant forward to look at it.

Her gasp as she recognised the handwriting in the distinctive violet ink echoed his exclamation when she was clearly illuminated for the first time.

'Sophia!' she hissed, and didn't know whether to burst into maniacal laughter or floods of tears when she realised what her sister had done.

'Ella?' he exclaimed, clearly shocked. 'Ella Buchan? What are *you* doing here?'

'What am *I* doing here?' she repeated. 'I live here, Seth. This is the *Buchan*'s Croft—' she stressed the correct pronunciation '—and since Sophia married in March, I am the last remaining Buchan.'

Ella stepped back into the cottage, opening the door wider to invite him into the warmth. There was no point in leaving him standing on the doorstep any longer, not now that she knew her wretched sister had deliberately sent Seth up to see her.

She should have expected Sophia to find some means of having her own way. All their lives she had been pulling rank as the older sister and the fact that she was now a married woman didn't seem to have made any difference—probably made things worse, in fact.

'But… How long have you been living here? No one seemed to know where you'd gone. Where are you working now?' The questions were tumbling out of him without giving her a chance to reply, but at least they were telling her that Sophia hadn't primed him before he'd come up here.

If she'd thought about it logically, she'd have realised that her sister was far too Machiavellian to have done that. All she'd needed to do had been to set the scene by sending Seth up to see her. That would guarantee that little sister Ella had to 'sort her life out' just as Sophia had been advising her for months.

Seth was standing there with his coat and scarf still on but apparently totally unaware of his surroundings, his eyes riveted to her face almost as if he was expecting her to disappear at any moment.

A sudden sharp ring took Ella by surprise. For a moment she couldn't think what it was, then remembered the bread dough waiting to be cooked.

'Excuse me but I've got to see to that,' she said as she hastily turned towards the fireplace. If she was lucky she could get her brain to work in the few moments the task would take.

'In that case, I'll bring those boxes in from the porch before they get buried under the snow,' he said after an interminable pause.

For a moment she'd thought he was going to insist on some immediate answers but the alternative was almost worse. The fact that he was even now carrying his belongings inside was bringing home to her the fact that, thanks to her sister's scheming, the one man she'd never wanted to see again was actually here, in her house. And, thanks to the dreadful weather, he was going to have to stay here at least until tomorrow morning.

She hurriedly bent to her task, raking the glowing embers out of the cloam oven before she slid the pans of perfectly risen dough into position and shut the door.

Automatically, she reached for the timer and set it again, wondering as she heard it begin to tick the minutes away how different her life was going to be by the time it rang again.

She wrapped her arms around herself as the front door opened again, tucking her hands up inside the ends of the baggy sleeves as the wind whistled across the room and straight up the chimney.

'Where do you want me to put these?' He gestured with a nod of his head towards the box he was carrying. 'It seems to be tins and packets. Staple items.'

'Through here.' She turned to open the door on the other side of the fireplace, nervousness setting her chattering. 'Granny always called it the scullery. The butler sink is still here but the old wash copper's been replaced with a machine—not that Granny saw the need for using it when she was only washing for one, but Dad insisted she wasn't to do the sheets and towels by hand any more.'

She had to stop when she ran out of breath and gestured silently for him to put the box on the battle-scarred wooden table against one wall.

Equally silently he obeyed, then paused to look around, his eyes taking in everything from the beamed ceiling that scarcely cleared his head to the handcrafted cupboards along one wall and the flagstoned floor.

Ella found she was almost holding her breath while she waited for his reaction to his simple surroundings. It was certainly very different from anything a top-flight obstetrics and gynaecology consultant would choose to live in.

Then he smiled. It was little more than a brief curving of a mouth that never smiled enough but it sent a shaft of warmth straight to her vulnerable heart.

'It's amazing,' he said softly, his eyes going back to her as she hovered anxiously in the doorway. 'Apart from the fridge and washing machine lurking in that corner you could almost imagine you'd stepped back in time. Is the whole croft the same?'

'More or less…apart from the sinful luxury of the tiniest bathroom in the Western world.'

'Thank God for that,' he exclaimed fervently. 'I suddenly wondered if there was still a…what were they called? At the bottom of the garden.'

'A privy? There is,' she informed him with a straight face, only breaking into a smile when she saw his look of horror. 'No longer in use, though,' she added, wickedly long seconds later.

The flash of humour in his eyes promised retribution but when he approached her it was only to make his way towards the remaining pile of bags and boxes.

He paused in mid-stride and whirled to face her, almost cannoning into her as she followed him across the room.

'Dammit, Ella, this isn't going to work,' he exclaimed, taking a hasty step out of her way as he raked a long-fingered hand through his hair. 'I came up here expecting to spend the next two weeks in an isolated little cottage of some sort. I certainly didn't expect to find you here and I want to know what's going on.'

'Going on?' It had sounded almost like an accusation but what was *she* guilty of?

'Well, obviously you got your sister to set me up, so what I want to know is what you're hoping to get out of it? If it's just another one-night stand you wanted, we certainly didn't have to come all this way for it. If you'd let me know you were interested, perhaps we could have arranged for a two-week stay in a comfortable hotel somewhere.'

'Seth!' The unexpectedness of his attack had left her almost speechless, apart from the fact that it was totally unfair. She wasn't the one who had—

'Of course! Stupid me! You don't go in for anything as long as two weeks. Just the one night after your sister's wedding and then, when I came back, you'd disappeared off the face of the earth.' He was so angry that his eyes were almost shooting sparks at her but that didn't stop her from retaliating with all the fire of her redhead's nature.

'*I* wasn't the one who disappeared after one night, or have you got a more convenient memory than I have?' She gave a mirthless laugh as the memories of that fateful day began to scroll their disjointed way through her head. She'd been trying to block them out for month after miserable month and still hadn't managed it.

'In case you really have forgotten what happened, let me remind you of the salient facts,' she snapped fiercely, holding one hand up to count them off, finger by finger.

'One—we danced at my sister's wedding. Two—we ended up in bed together. Three—*you* had disappeared by the time I woke up the next morning. Four—by the time I went back on duty it was announced that you had gone on some sort of hastily organised leave with no date given for your return. Now,' she continued when she'd drawn in a hasty breath and planted her fists combatively on her hips, 'correct me if I've missed anything out, but I'm almost certain that nowhere in that series of events was there any mention on your part that you'd even enjoyed the encounter in the first place, let alone that you were interested in repeating it.'

His lips had been pressed into a thin line and his hands had been balled into tight fists when she'd started, but by the time she finished his arms were hanging limp at his sides, his eyes riveted on the front of her baggy jumper.

She glanced down to see that she'd planted her hands on her hips as she'd harangued him, and the gesture had drawn her clothing against the burgeoning evidence of her heavily pregnant state.

'My God! Ella, you're pregnant!' he breathed, clearly shocked.

'Well, I'm glad to see that all those years of training weren't wasted,' she retorted acidly, just as the timer rang again.

It didn't take more than a minute to turn the loaves round to ensure they baked evenly, but it was long enough for her to regret her rudeness.

There had been two of them in that hotel room that night and that meant it had been just as much her fault as his that they hadn't taken any steps to prevent her getting pregnant.

She straightened up from her task, knowing that she had to apologise, but before she could speak he beat her to it.

'So, who's the father? I hadn't heard you'd got married but, then, once you left the hospital you were outside the scope of the gossip grapevine.' He stopped suddenly, as though struck by a sudden thought. 'Is this place big enough to have guests to stay? Won't your husband have something to say about your sister dumping an old colleague of yours on him?'

For a moment Ella didn't know whether she was going to laugh or cry but ended up determined to do neither.

'You *stupid* man!' she exclaimed shrilly as all those months of wondering and hurting finally boiled over. 'I'm not married. I have never been married and I have no intention of ever getting married. Furthermore, whether you believe it or not, you are the only man I've ever slept with, but to save you wasting your money on DNA testing I'll tell you here and now that I won't be asking you for a single penny to raise this child. At least you'll go away from here secure in the knowledge that I have no intention of using the baby to destroy your marriage.'

The last words were still quivering in the bread-scented room when reaction began to set in.

This was not how she'd dreamed of telling Seth that he was going to be a father.

In her dreams his marriage didn't exist and he'd come to her telling her that he'd missed her dreadfully and couldn't bear to live without her.

In her dreams he'd told her that he loved her and the baby they'd made that magical night, and would take care of them for ever.

In her dreams he came to her and wrapped her in loving arms while he kissed her. He didn't stand on the other side of the room like a statue carved out of granite with his eyes burning into her like hot coals.

For a moment she just stood there with her hands resting protectively over the prominent bulge of her pregnancy, wondering why everything had gone so wrong. When she'd first met him she'd thought he was something so special. How could she have been so mistaken?

They had been working together for several months before the fateful day of her sister's wedding, time in which she'd believed they'd been getting to know each other. Only she hadn't known him at all. Hadn't known that he'd been hiding such a monstrous secret until it had been far too late to stop herself falling in love with him.

She was still glaring at him after her outburst, but the longer she looked the more she began to notice about his appearance.

He'd changed since she'd seen him last. There was a sprinkling of grey at his temples that hadn't been there before and he looked thinner, almost as if he'd been ill.

There was a subtle difference in the expression in his eyes, too. A year ago their polished steel had had the intensity of lasers where now they seemed almost…almost defeated.

He doesn't look happy, she thought with a strange ache around her heart.

Startled by the burgeoning emotion she'd vowed to dismiss for ever, she suddenly realised that in spite of everything she was as much in love with him as she'd ever been.

Then to her utter mortification she burst into tears.

CHAPTER TWO

FROM the first moment she saw him, Ella felt as though a light had been switched on inside her.

'Seth Gifford,' she whispered as she walked away after their first introduction, loving the feel of the words in her mouth.

Somehow she just knew that she had met the man who was going to be the most important part of her life, and she was filled with an almost giddy excitement.

It wasn't enough that she'd just landed the job of her dreams. After waiting twenty-seven years and nearly giving up hope, she'd met the man of her dreams, too. What was more, she was almost certain she'd seen an answering spark of attraction in his eyes that had nothing to do with the fact that she was a well-qualified midwife.

'Is there anything else you want to see?' her guide asked as they continued on their way along the light and airy corridor towards the delivery suites.

A swift sideways glance at her new colleague reassured her that Carol didn't seem to have noticed anything amiss in her reaction to their obs and gyn consultant and she breathed a sigh of relief. That was not the way she wanted to start to build up a relationship in the department.

'I'll probably have dozens of questions,' she answered with a laugh. 'But you've told me so much in the last half-hour that I can't tell what's stuck yet.'

'I know what you mean,' Carol commiserated. 'Every obs and gyn department does the same basic job but there are always differences in their routines when you move to another hospital.' She paused to throw Ella a speculative look. 'What do you think so far? Are you going to like us enough to stay?'

I'd stay just for the pleasure of seeing Seth Gifford every day, she heard a little voice say inside her head, and swiftly squashed it. 'This is pretty much my ideal job,' she admitted candidly, not seeing the point of beating around the bush. 'I've always wanted to work somewhere that was at the forefront of all aspects of human fertility, and to come here, where there are so many inter-departmental links, is perfect.'

The understanding smile on Carol's face encouraged her to continue enthusiastically.

'I'll be learning, too, because I'll be able to see everything from perfectly straightforward deliveries of naturally achieved pregnancies to those that would never have happened without medical assistance. And then there's the staff. I only met some of them when I came for my interview, but everyone's been very welcoming, right up to the top man.'

'Top man?' Carol questioned. 'Oh, you mean Mr Gifford. He's not exactly the top man because we share Professor den Haag with St Augustine's, and Mr Crossman, our other consultant, has about ten years' seniority, but he *is* all our own.'

Ella suddenly found herself longing to ask Carol for details about Seth and that shook her. She'd never allowed anyone or anything to interfere with her job before, and she wasn't going to let her hormones get in the way now. It might be the first time they'd really sat up and taken notice of anyone, but that was her own problem.

'So, what is the atmosphere like in the department? Does everyone get on well?' she asked as her guide finally took her into the comfortable atmosphere of the staff lounge to make them a coffee. Carol had warned, laughingly, that sitting down would probably be the signal for dozens of patients to turn up in complicated labour, but they'd deemed it worth the risk. Midwifery was definitely one of the less predictable specialties and they all learned early on in their training to grab the chance of a break with both hands.

'Actually, we *do* all get on reasonably well,' Carol confirmed thoughtfully. 'You'll always get those who don't pull their weight quite as willingly as others but here they seem to be balanced by others who always do their share and more.'

'Doesn't that lead to friction?'

'Oh, there's the occasional flare-up to make the slackers pull their socks up, but it's generally fairly good-natured.'

'What about the bigwigs? What are they like to work with?' She hadn't been able to resist asking after all.

'Professor den Haag is wonderful. He's a big blond gorgeous teddy bear of a man who loves his work every bit as much as he loves his wife and family. They've got six children already. Three sets of twins!'

Ella blinked. She couldn't imagine how any woman coped with *one* set, let alone three.

'Wow! Gluttons for punishment!' she exclaimed. 'What about Mr Crossman? I met him briefly at my interview but he was called into theatre for an emergency Caesarean almost as soon as we shook hands.'

'He's a quiet man, not much older than the professor but seems much more middle-aged somehow. Steady and hardworking but doesn't seem to have much rapport with his patients—the adult ones, that is. He adores babies, though. He's just become a grandfather for the first time so he'll probably trap you in a corner with the latest photos when he finds he's got a new victim to show them to.'

'I've been warned!' Ella chuckled. 'And what about Mr Gifford?' Finally, she'd asked about the one person she really wanted to know about.

'Well, what can I tell you?' Carol said with a shrug and a roll of her eyes. 'Obviously, he's totally gorgeous. The archetypal tall, dark and handsome with those lovely velvety grey eyes, added to which he's brilliant at his job and excellent with all his patients. But other than that, there isn't much to tell. He hasn't been here very long—probably nearly six months now. He seems to keep himself very much to himself outside his duty hours and that's as much as we know so far.'

'That's quite amazing, knowing what hospital grapevines are like,' Ella commented, unaccountably disappointed not to have learned anything of a more personal nature about the man who had jump-started her female hormones at last. 'Usually everyone knows everything, *including* his inside leg length, within the first twenty-four hours of a good-looking man joining the staff.'

Carol was still laughing as she got up to answer the phone but her smile had faded by the time the call ended.

'Damn!' she muttered with a scowl and tipped the rest of her coffee down the sink.

'Problem?' Ella was already on her feet and giving her pale blue tunic top a tug to straighten the hem over her hips.

'One of our assisted pregnancies has started bleeding. Her husband's bringing her in now.'

'Oh, dear. How far along is she? Enough for the baby to survive?' Automatically Ella found herself following Carol out into the department, her own coffee unceremoniously dumped with barely a pang of regret.

'No chance at all. She's not even reached the end of the first trimester yet. And this time I really thought we'd cracked it for them.' Carol sounded really upset for the couple.

'You sound as if you know them well. I take it they've been coming for a while?'

'Too long,' she confirmed darkly. 'I first met them when they were going through all the tests to find out why she wasn't conceiving. She'd had problems with an IUD when they were first married but hadn't realised that the infection had affected her Fallopian tubes. Both tubes were so badly scarred that finally it was decided that their only option was IVF. This is their third attempt.'

Ella had come across such cases at her last hospital and her heart went out to the couple. She couldn't imagine what it must be like to want to start a family only to discover that you would never achieve it without medical intervention. The fact that this was already their third attempt was witness to this couple's determination to succeed.

Unfortunately, she mused while they waited for Mira to arrive, sometimes all the determination in the world was not enough to ensure success. Would they be one of the unlucky ones who were fated never to have a child of their own?

'She's one of Mr Gifford's cases,' Carol announced, scanning the top page of the case notes as she came back into the examination room where Ella had been checking the range of supplies to hand. 'Could you page him for me? The numbers are listed on the wall phone for convenience. I've already contacted the ultrasound technician and checked the availability of a bed in case she needs to be admitted.'

Ella had barely put the phone back in its cradle after logging the page when it rang again.

'Winston Ward,' she said automatically, completely forgetting that this wasn't her old hospital, then hastily corrected herself. 'I'm sorry. That's not right. It's…what *is* the name of the obs and gyn department, Carol?' she hissed over her shoulder, totally flustered by her mistake. If she hadn't been thinking about Seth Gifford she'd have had her mind on her job.

'I take it that's Ella,' said a dark brown velvet voice in her ear. 'It's Seth Gifford here. Somebody paged me.'

'Yes. I—I did…or rather Carol asked me to,' she stammered, completely thrown by the tremor of awareness that spiralled through her at the sound of his voice. She thought she could even hear amusement in his tone.

'Mira Connolly is on her way in,' she continued, hastily dragging her wayward thoughts back to the important matter in hand. 'Apparently she's bleeding.'

'Damn!' she heard him say forcefully. 'I'll be there in a couple of minutes. I expect Carol's organised the ultrasound?'

'Yes. And a bed in case she needs to be admitted.'

'Well done.'

The sharp click in her ear told her that he'd cut the connection but it took her a second to relinquish her hold on the receiver.

'How soon can he be here?' Carol prompted.

'He's already on his way, by the sound of it. He doesn't waste time on small talk, does he?'

'You'd be surprised,' she argued. 'I've never seen him watching the clock when a patient needs reassurance.'

The sound of the lift arriving had both of them craning their necks around the doorjamb to see who was arriving. A wheelchair emerged at speed expertly wielded by a porter.

The tearstained woman huddled in it was obviously their patient while the tall man following them, his thinning blond hair wildly dishevelled and devastation in his eyes, was equally obviously her husband.

'This way, Mick,' Carol called when the porter paused briefly to look both ways along the corridor. 'We're all ready in here.'

'Is Mr Gifford here?' the woman demanded tearfully as soon as she caught sight of the two of them. 'I need to see Mr Gifford. He'll be able to do something, I know he will. I *can't* lose this baby. Not this time!' She dissolved into racking sobs that continued right through her transfer onto the examining couch. Even Carol's repeated assurances that the consultant was on his way couldn't comfort her.

Ella wasn't sure what she expected Seth to do when he arrived but it certainly wasn't the way he walked straight across to sit on the edge of the couch and wrap a comforting arm around the patient's shoulders.

'Hush, Mira,' he murmured. 'Hush, now. You don't even know whether there's anything to cry about. You haven't even given me a chance to check yet.'

'But…but I'm b-bleeding again. I've l-lost the b-baby again. I know I have!'

'Mira, listen to me,' he demanded sternly, deliberately holding her gaze. 'Have I ever lied to you?'

'N-no.' She shook her head miserably.

'Well, I won't start now. Obviously as you're bleeding there *is* a chance that you've lost your baby. You've been through this often enough to know that. But, until I've checked you over, none of us can know for sure. Even women who aren't on IVF sometimes have intermittent bleeding for one reason or another, and then go on to have perfectly normal healthy babies.'

She nodded, but Ella knew the poor woman didn't really believe it.

'Well, I hope you trust me enough to know that I'll always tell you the truth, whatever it is,' Seth said softly as he straightened up off the side of the examining couch, relinquishing his position with a gesture to her husband to take his place.

Ella was certain that the rest of them in the room had been trying to look as if they were busy with something else to give her the semblance of privacy, but she knew that she'd been riveted by Seth's compassion while he'd been calming Mira down. She certainly hadn't noticed the arrival of the ultrasound technician.

'How long ago did you empty your bladder?' the motherly woman asked quietly as she began to set up the equipment, switching on the computerised display and thoughtfully warming the probe.

'Actually, I need to go now,' Mira admitted, looking fearfully at the blank screen that would soon display the presence or absence of the baby in her womb. 'Should I go before you start?'

'It's not necessary for you to go anywhere,' she said soothingly. 'It's actually better if your bladder is full. We can get a better picture.'

Ella stepped forward to help rearrange Mira's clothing to expose her abdomen, draping her with a towel so that the conductive jelly didn't make a mess.

'Lie very still now,' the technician warned as she took the probe in a smooth sweep across the pale skin of her lower abdomen.

Ella couldn't see the screen from her position so had to content herself with watching Seth's expression.

He started off with his dark brows drawn together to form a deep furrow above his nose as he concentrated on the shadows and blurs that the screen would display. At one point he murmured something to the technician, his grey eyes piercingly intent as he pointed at something on the screen, and Ella found herself holding her breath.

In spite of the number of people in the room and the hum of the equipment, she was certain she could have heard the proverbial pin drop while they waited for the verdict. When he straightened up and turned to face Mira again the expression on his face had hardly changed but some sixth sense told her that the news was going to be good.

'I don't think you've ever seen one of these scans before, have you?' he began conversationally, pulling the trolley full of electronic gadgetry over slightly so that his patient could see the picture on the screen more easily without having to move her position.

'This is your uterus,' he continued, tracing the outline on the screen. 'And this dark tadpole, just here, is your baby. The head is smaller than the width of two of your fingers and from the top of the head to its little rump is less than the length of your little finger.'

They all heard Mira swallow before she could force herself to speak, her eyes glued to the tiny shadow on the screen.

'Is it still alive?' she whispered fearfully, clutching so tightly to her husband's hand that his fingers were turning white. He seemed to be too engrossed in the screen to even notice.

'See for yourself,' Seth urged with a nod to the technician to run the scan again. 'That was a still frame you were looking at, while this is what is happening inside you while we're looking at it. Can you see that little fluttering movement?'

'Yes,' they agreed breathlessly, still without taking their eyes off the screen.

'That's your baby's heart beating inside you, and the last time I checked an ultrasound, only live babies had hearts that beat that strongly.'

Mira burst into tears, but this time they were accompanied by a tremulous smile. Ella was hard put not to join her, concentrating on wiping up the jelly and righting Mira's clothing while she regained her composure.

'So why was she bleeding?' Mira's husband finally asked, obviously very close to tears himself.

'We might never know,' Seth admitted candidly. 'Most people don't realise that only one in six of *normally* conceived babies ever survive to birth, and the proportion is even lower for assisted pregnancies like yours. But if I were to hazard a guess, I would say that Mira just lost the twin.'

'The twin?' he echoed, obviously too befuddled to think clearly.

'You remember that we put two embryos back in when we did the implantation?' Seth prompted patiently. 'It's possible that both of them actually started to grow, but that one of them has just failed for some reason.'

'What about the one that's left? What are his chances?'

'I'm afraid I'm not in the business of fortune-telling,' he said as kindly as he could. 'All we can do is wait and see.' He glanced back at Mira who was now gazing at the print the technician had made for her of that little tadpole with the beating heart.

'I'd like to keep her in overnight,' he added softly for the husband's ears. 'I think she'll probably be calmer knowing we're close at hand, even if there's really nothing we can do at this stage.'

It didn't take long for the arrangements to be made and even though Ella had never met the woman before, she found herself crossing her fingers that this story would have a happy ending.

Seth had obviously been called to the department from some other task, but there was no sign that he was in a hurry to return to it. In spite of the fact that he had already done his part in explaining what was going on, he waited in the unit until Mira had been settled into bed.

'Make sure you get a good night's sleep, now,' he warned when he stuck his head around the door. 'Stress won't do any of you any good and, with any luck, you're going to need every bit of your strength when that little one arrives in another six months.'

He glanced at Ella and her pulse gave a silly skip at the intensity she saw in those clear grey eyes, especially when they lingered for an extra moment.

'You can page me if you're worried about anything,' he said quietly. 'I don't think there'll be any problems, but I won't be far away if you need me.'

She nodded, but even before he disappeared down the corridor she was silently kicking herself. There might have been a special intensity in his gaze when he'd looked at her but it was obviously purely as a result of his concern for his patient. There was nothing personal in it at all.

'That'll teach you to let the attraction get out of hand,' she muttered crossly to herself as she set the examination room to rights. 'Just because there are lights, bells and whistles going off inside you whenever he's around doesn't mean that he feels the same way. Grow up!'

The trouble was, these were all the symptoms of growing up that she'd missed out on when she'd been a teenager. She'd seen her classmates and even her sister go through the clammy hands, racing pulse and gooey eyes stage over the boys without ever suffering a hint of it herself.

Unfortunately, it looked as if she was coming down with a massive case of it now.

'If you've finished in here, would you like to see if you can do anything with this?' Carol asked, hefting the scruffy-looking cardboard box in her arms.

'It depends what "this" is,' Ella said, taking a wary peep inside the flaps. 'Oh! Christmas decorations! I'd almost forgotten how close it was getting. I'd be delighted to have a go. Any guidelines?'

'Well, the hospital usually puts a big tree up in the main reception area and threads lights through the ones either side of the entrance outside. They give us a smaller one for the central reception area dividing the two halves of this unit but it's up to us to do the decorating of that and the wards. That box you're holding is the treasure trove of almost every bit of tatty tinsel from the first Christmas since the hospital opened this wing.'

'It doesn't look as if there's enough in here to make a cheerful show in *one* room, let alone the whole department,' Ella said with a grimace. The closer she examined it, the tattier everything appeared. It also seemed as if it had all been squashed flat when it had been piled in the box at the end of last Christmas.

'Well, I'll leave it all in your capable hands,' Carol said, beating a suspiciously hasty retreat.

'Gee, thanks!' Ella muttered as she made her way to the staff lounge, wondering what on earth she was going to be able to achieve with so little to work with. Some of their patients were in for such a long time for bed rest that they would need the department brightened up for the festive season. It was bad enough to endure months of uncertainty with a threatened miscarriage without having to stare at the same old walls while the rest of the hospital was decorated in a celebratory mood.

'Problem?' enquired a dark brown velvet voice and Ella nearly dropped the box.

'Oh, I'm sorry,' she gasped when Seth had to grab to prevent the contents cascading onto the floor. 'I didn't realise there was anyone in here and you made me jump.'

Well, it was nearly true. She hadn't known he was here and her reaction to hearing his voice right beside her had nearly caused her to drop her burden.

'In which case, *I'm* sorry,' he said sincerely as he relieved her of the unwieldy carton and placed it on the nearest coffee-table. 'Am I allowed to ask what this is?'

'Feel free to have a look,' she offered, frustrated to hear how breathless she sounded. He was going to think she was some sort of brainless twit at this rate. It really was time she got herself under control.

'Ah,' he said solemnly. 'I can quite understand why you were looking glum. I take it this is the departmental box of decorations.'

'I hope it isn't the sum total of festive cheer for the whole hospital or we might all be in for a pretty miserable time,' Ella said wryly. 'Any suggestions as to how these can be rejuvenated? At the moment they're more likely to induce deep depression.'

'Hmm.' He held up a very ragged-looking fairy and raised an eyebrow. 'I see what you mean. I can't imagine *this* granting anybody's wishes.'

'The rest of it isn't any better. Look at it,' she groaned. 'How is *that* supposed to cheer up the whole department, including a tree in the central reception area?'

'The short answer is that it won't,' he said, his voice suddenly decisive. 'I've got an idea. Will you come for a quick walk through the department and give me an idea of what we need to do this properly?'

'What do you mean—properly?' she said warily.

'I don't know exactly. Not stuff because they have that and I presume that the kids mums in here have their own stu

He looked up to glance around spartan room they were standing in ing her with that surprisingly inte gaze.

'I'm not thinking about anything ov top. Just something fairly simple—and ful—that can be repeated with variations each area.'

'You mean the same sort of decorations the doors and windows of each room, or over each bed, but in a different colour scheme for each area.'

'That sort of thing, yes. Do you think it would work?'

There was an almost boyish enthusiasm in his voice that surprised her, having seen how seriously he seemed to treat life.

'I think it would be perfect!' she exclaimed, completely bowled over by this unexpected side to him. 'Much better than tired tinsel that

…f years ago. The …it?'

…had the im- …going on …again in a

… times of duties …rhaps we could go …at we can find.'

… go shopping…together?'

…athless again, hardly able to …e was hearing. She'd only met … few hours ago and it had just … as if he was suggesting the two of … go shopping for Christmas decorations …gether.

'I don't see that there's any alternative, unless you can think of a way to magically resuscitate that lot.' He hitched a dismissive thumb at the box. 'I'm prepared to foot the bill for the new stuff if you'll come with me to give some input on the selection. Deal?'

His final word almost sounded like a challenge and there was a suspicious glint in his eyes as he held his hand out towards her.

'OK. Deal,' she agreed rashly and put her hand in his.

That first contact between them sent a shiver through her and her heart seemed to take an extra beat before it settled into a faster rhythm.

'So when are you free? This afternoon?'

Ella couldn't think. Not with her hand still firmly held in his. Had he forgotten it was there or was he holding it hostage until he'd pinned her down to a specific time?

'Um. I think so. Yes. I've been rostered for a short day, as it's my first day here, in case there was any paperwork still to be sorted out. I know there isn't because I went to the personnel department yesterday after I'd picked up my uniforms.'

'So, what time shall we meet and where? Do you know the area at all? Do you know if there are any shops around here that specialise in things like Christmas decorations? It's not something I've had much experience with buying.'

She gave her hand a little tug and for the briefest second he seemed strangely reluctant to release her, then let go of her hand with a jerk as though suddenly remembering where they were and what he was doing.

'I'm due to finish at three, but—'

'But that will depend on whether you're in the middle of a delivery,' he finished for her. 'You don't have to tell me how it works.' He thought for a minute. 'I'll come up at three to see how the land lies and we can take it from there. Did you drive to work this morning or shall we go in my car?'

Ella's head was still whirling with the speed of events long after he'd left the room. Thank goodness the department was so quiet. She wasn't at all sure that she would have been capable of concentrating on managing even the most straightforward delivery.

Even the simple task of wandering around the department to get an idea of just how many doors and windows there were seemed to be beyond her. It wasn't until she nearly tripped over her own feet that she finally got her head on straight and began to think logically. She even managed to take a wicked delight in weaving a web of suspense about what she was up to, carefully keeping Seth's part in the plans strictly to herself.

It nearly drove the rest of the staff mad as they pestered her for details. It was only when a couple of them cornered her during her lunch-break that she realised that the decorating of the department was an annual bugbear that everyone tried to palm off to whoever didn't run fast enough in the opposite direction.

As the newest member of staff she had been a sitting duck.

'Well, this duck won't quack,' she murmured to herself, knowing that her mysterious grins and misleading hints were putting everyone off the scent. As if she'd actually intended taking the tinsel home to iron the crumpled sections!

On the other hand, the patients were thoroughly enjoying the situation, taking an almost evil glee in winding the rest of the staff up for her.

As she'd gone into each room, from the four-bedded wards to the single-occupancy rooms, she'd sworn each inmate to secrecy before explaining what she was doing.

Several of them had offered suggestions, either of decorating schemes or of good places to find the decorations at a reasonable price.

By the time three o'clock came around without a potential new arrival in sight, Ella had a notepad full of diagrams, measurements and totals and was ready to go.

The sight of Seth's dark head appearing round the door of the staff lounge was enough to double her heart rate, but she determinedly told herself that it was just a result of their subterfuge.

'You're ready,' he said with a satisfied nod. 'I'll get the car and meet you down by the entrance to the staff car park.'

'Um…' She paused, suddenly tongue-tied because she didn't know what to call him. 'Ah, Mr Gifford, I don't know—'

'Ella, it's Seth,' he interrupted quietly. 'I'm only Mr Gifford in front of the patients. OK?'

'OK.' She swallowed, surprised by how intimate it felt to be invited to use his first name.

'I was only going to say that I don't know what your car looks like.'

'It's white. A BMW, 3-series.'

She couldn't help the grin.

'What's wrong with that?' His forehead pleated in a swift frown.

'I wouldn't know a 3-series from a moon-rocket,' she explained with a chuckle. 'But I do know what the BMW logo looks like on the bonnet and I know the colour white.'

He raised his eyes in typical male exasperation and one corner of his mouth actually lifted in a wry grin before he raised a hand in farewell and let the door close behind him.

CHAPTER THREE

'BRR! I hadn't realised it was so cold out here!' Ella exclaimed through chattering teeth as she slid hastily into Seth's car.

'And the forecast is for worse to come,' he warned as he leaned forward to turn the heater up to maximum then glanced across at her, obviously checking that she'd fastened her seat belt before he set off. 'Apparently, there's some local man who's been doing his own forecast for the last forty years or so—gets it right more often than the pundits with their electronics, by all accounts—and he reckons it's going to be another long cold wet winter.'

'Thanks! That's just what I needed to hear! Couldn't he at least have sweetened the pill by mentioning a few brief spells of sunshine and unseasonable warmth?'

He laughed. 'Sorry. Not a balmy breeze in sight. Still, what are you worried about? You work in a fully heated hospital, warm enough for people to wander about in their shirtsleeves all year round.'

'That's the trouble. It makes coming out into the cold so much more of a shock to the system.' Almost as much of a shock as finding herself sitting side by side with Seth Gifford in the intimate confines of his quietly luxurious car. Thank goodness they had the weather and other allied subjects to talk about or she'd be sitting here tongue-tied.

'I'm sure that central heating has a lot to do with all these flu epidemics we keep having each year,' she continued hastily, not wanting the silence to stretch too long in case she leapt into the void with something embarrassing. 'My grandmother always maintained that people aren't nearly so hardy as they used to be when they lived in virtually unheated houses.'

'Tell that to the ones who died of the flu pandemic just after the First World War,' he argued. 'Twice as many died of that in a matter of weeks as were killed in the four years of the war itself, and none of them were living with central heating.'

'I know, but they didn't have access to the Health Service or the variety of drugs we have now, so there would have been far more people in the "at risk" category.'

'True,' he conceded, more than half his concentration on manoeuvring the car into a parking space in the car park attached to the shopping centre. 'There *are* fewer deaths from flu these days than back in 1918, but... Oh, for goodness' sake, what are we debating this for?' he exclaimed with disbelief clear in his voice as he turned to face her with the keys in his hand. 'We're on our way to buy Christmas decorations, so let's declare a truce.'

'A Christmas truce, like they had in the trenches during the War?' she proposed cheekily.

'Does that mean that hostilities could break out again as soon as the last mince pie has been eaten?' Seth frowned as he pretended to consider the idea seriously. 'Still, a Christmas truce that starts now means that there should be at least two weeks of peace, so I accept.'

He held out his hand and without a moment's thought Ella took it.

It didn't matter that she was wearing gloves this time, the effect of the contact between them was just as strong and just as startling. What was going on here?

His hand tightened briefly around hers and her eyes flew up to meet his. He was frowning again, his gaze flicking from her face to their joined hands and back again before he suddenly released his hold on her.

'Well,' he said, his voice rather too hearty for the enclosed space as he turned away to open his door, 'I hope you know where we're going to be able to get these things because I haven't a clue.'

So, what happened there? she mused as he strode off to fetch a parking ticket from the dispenser. It didn't seem very likely that he had felt the same reaction that she had, there'd certainly been no evidence of it in his expression. Dear God, she hoped he hadn't seen something in her own face. It would be just too embarrassing if he knew how strongly he affected her.

'Time for a little self-control,' she muttered grimly as she found herself watching his long legs eating up the distance as he returned with the ticket in his hand, then deliberately looked away to let herself out of the car. 'That's the last time you let your stupid hormones get the better of you.'

'Ready to go?' he said as he stuck the ticket to his windscreen and shut the door. The car bleeped obligingly when he pressed the button to lock it. 'I'm in the mood to spend some money on glitter and glitz, so lead the way!'

Two and a half hours later they were both laden down with parcels, none of which had anything to do with decorating the department.

'Well, all I can say is thank goodness that shop was willing to deliver!' Ella exclaimed breathlessly as she struggled to untangle her fingers from various loops and strings. 'We'd never have been able to carry all those decorations as well as this lot.'

'You didn't mind me hijacking you like that?' he asked with a frown. 'I did ask you if you'd help me choose some gifts for my brother's family.'

'I didn't mind at all,' she said with a laugh. 'How else was I going to be able to get free transport to get this lot home? I've actually been able to find something for absolutely everyone on my list, and there's still two weeks to go till Christmas. That's an all-time record for me. I'm usually one of those demented souls racing around as the shops are locking up on Christmas Eve.'

'What? You?' Seth said with every evidence of amazement. 'Calmness and order personified actually gets into a flap about buying Christmas presents? I don't believe it. You've ordered me about like a seasoned field marshal barking at his troops. You knew exactly where we needed to go and what we needed to buy.'

'That was just the decorations and I was only so well organised because I'd made a list of everything we needed. It's different with presents for family and friends. There are either too many choices or I haven't got a clue what to get.'

'Well, I shall certainly be taking all the credit for your inspired suggestions this year. My lot aren't going to know what's hit them when they don't get the usual box of chocolates and bottle of booze.'

He slammed the boot down on the dozens of bags and packages as she let herself into the passenger side and sank into the blissfully comfortable upholstery.

'Oh, that feels so good,' she groaned aloud. 'Excuse me moaning, but my feet are killing me and I only worked a short day today.'

'You probably did several miles walking up and down corridors and stairs, though,' he pointed out as they left the car park into the darkness that had fallen while they'd been cocooned in the artificial daylight of the shopping precinct. 'With a hospital that size, it's like running round a small town to get anywhere.'

'That's true. And it doesn't help if you don't know exactly where you're going. I probably did a few extra miles just trying to find my way around.'

Silence fell between them but this time she was quite content to let it grow. Somehow, their time together seemed to have taken the edge off her awareness of him and she could almost persuade herself that the new ease between them was the start of a good friendship that would develop with time.

She gave him directions and all too soon he'd drawn up outside the old Victorian house in which she was renting a little bedsit and she found herself very reluctant to end their time together.

It took her a moment or two to screw up her courage but by the time he'd helped her to carry her share of the booty to the front door she was ready.

'It wouldn't take me long to have a meal ready—nothing cordon bleu but definitely something better than microwave hell. Would you like to join me…to say thank you for helping me with my Christmas shopping today?'

She'd gabbled her way to the end of her invitation then waited breathlessly for his reply. She was convinced he was going to accept until he glanced at his watch.

'Is that really the time?' he said with a strange expression on his face. 'I'd completely lost track. I'm sorry, Ella,' he said hastily, almost as if he wasn't really aware of what he was saying as he deposited the handful of bags he'd carried for her. 'I've got to go. An appointment…a meeting I'd already arranged to go to. If I don't go now, I'm going to be late.'

He was halfway down the cracked concrete path before he half-turned to call over his shoulder, 'Thank you for the offer. And thank you, again, for helping me with the shopping.'

'You're welcome,' she called weakly, but her words were lost under the sound of the car unlocking to his command.

For some reason she stayed there watching as he climbed in and fastened his seat belt then started the engine, and was left feeling completely stupid with her hand raised to wave when he drove off without another glance in her direction.

'So much for rapport,' she muttered, her cheeks warm with embarrassment in spite of the chilly wind as she retrieved her packages and made her way to her room.

She tried to persuade herself that she really didn't care where he'd been going in such a hurry. After all, he was a very busy consultant and there could have been any number of meetings he'd been scheduled to attend.

'Except he wouldn't have suggested going out for a shopping trip if he still had meetings to go to. Surely he would have chosen another day?'

The only other possibility she could think of was that he'd already had a dinner date and had completely forgotten about it until she'd mentioned cooking for him.

Perhaps he had a girlfriend, partner or even a wife somewhere who was waiting for him with a home-cooked meal. The fact that the hospital didn't know anything about his private life didn't mean that he didn't have one, and the fact that the two of them had spent a couple of hours or so together didn't mean that he was duty bound to give her any more details than he'd told anyone else.

She started to unpack the presents she'd chosen so light-heartedly such a short time ago and then sighed. Somehow part of the pleasure had gone out of it although there was no logical reason why it should have.

Still, she couldn't find the enthusiasm to do any wrapping up tonight. That would have to be done another day—probably in a rush on Christmas Eve, as usual, she thought, then realised that even that brought Seth and his unexpected teasing to mind.

'Oh, stop it!' she growled and slouched against the edge of the sink while she waited for the kettle to boil. Instead of concerning herself over the possibility that the obs and gyn consultant had some gorgeous woman waiting for him at the end of each shift, she should be thinking about what she was going to eat.

She wouldn't bother to make the same effort just for herself as she would have done if she'd been sharing the meal with Seth…

'For heaven's sake! Don't start!' She reached for a couple of slices of bread and a small tin of baked beans from the cupboard. 'I'll have scrambled eggs and baked beans on toast with some fresh fruit to follow…and at least two cups of tea. But first I'll sort out a load of washing so it's in the machine while I'm eating and catching up on the news. Then

I'm having a bath and an early night because tomorrow I'll probably be run off my feet.'

'I must have jinxed myself last night,' Ella groaned. 'I had an early night in case we were busy today.'

'I reckon you jinxed the lot of us,' Serena complained as she slid her feet out of her shoes and wriggled her toes. 'I don't think I've ever seen the department this busy.'

'Except in September when all the Christmas and New Year babies start arriving,' Jo added. 'Don't you remember what that was like, nine months after all those Millennium parties? It was nearly as bad as all those people who tried to have the "first" Millennium baby.'

It had been the same story at Ella's last post and they all groaned in unison just as there was a knock at the staff lounge door.

'Excuse the interruption, ladies,' said the porter with a cheerful grin. 'Some of us don't have time to sit around with our feet up. We're rushing here, there and everywhere at everyone's beck and call. It's ''Fetch this, Mick. Deliver that, Mick,'' all day long.'

'Well, this time it's ''Get to the point, Mick,'' or we might be tempted to see if we can do something about that verbal diarrhoea,' Jo said with a pointed glare.

'Just thought I'd tell you how it is for us lesser mortals,' he said with a mock cringe. 'We could get hernias lugging great boxes like this around.' He pulled a wheelchair into view and expertly swung it into the room in spite of the fact that it was piled high with several boxes.

'Labels on each of them say they're for G. Buchan. Personal. Maternity.' He looked at them for help. 'So who's this G. Buchan, then? Doctor, nurse, midwife or patient?'

'Actually, they're for me,' Ella said as she scrambled to her feet. She was as mystified as the rest of them as to what it was about.

'*G.* Buchan?' Serena repeated. 'But you're called Ella.'

'It's a nickname. Short for Gabriella, courtesy of my Italian mother,' she explained absently as she tried to work out who had sent her the parcels and what they contained.

Suddenly she caught sight of the logo on the corner of the label and knew what they contained, and the quizzing about her unusual name faded into oblivion.

'Great! They've arrived!' she exclaimed with a whoop. 'Thanks, Mick.'

'You be careful how you lift them boxes. Could do yourself an injury,' he warned with a wink as he hefted the first one up out of the wheelchair as if it weighed at least a ton.

Ella picked the second one up and tucked it under her arm to take it across to the table to the accompaniment of a chorus of laughs when her colleagues realised just how little they weighed.

Mick gave them a cheeky wave and a grin as he wheeled the chair out and shut the door behind him.

'Anyone got a knife or a pair of scissors?' Ella asked as she tried to pick at the corner of the tape with a fingernail. 'This little lot is going to be a real tonic. I bet it'll even make us forget we're overworked and under-appreciated.'

'Do you know what it is?' Serena asked, her tired feet forgotten as curiosity got the better of her.

'Have you got a rich boyfriend?' Jo demanded as she attacked the tape on the second parcel with the handle of a teaspoon. 'And if so, has he got an even richer brother? *I* never get spectacular presents like this.'

'No boyfriend. No presents. This is a special delivery *to* the department, *for* the department.' Ella folded back the flaps on the first box with a flourish to reveal all the Christmas glitter and glitz anyone could have wished for.

'Wow! What's all this?' Serena demanded, as wide-eyed as any child. 'Where did it all come from?'

Suddenly they all had their hands in the boxes, gingerly lifting out the carefully packed layers.

'If you separate everything out into the different colours...perhaps we could stack them on chairs to keep them apart...' Ella might as well have saved her breath. They were all far too busy oohing and aahing.

'So they've arrived, then,' said that dark brown velvet voice and Ella's heart performed a triple somersault before she could catch her breath. After Seth's hasty departure last night she hadn't been certain how she would face him today.

'Do you need any help putting them up?' he offered, shrugging out of his suit jacket and draping it casually over the back of a chair before rolling up the sleeves of his shirt. 'I've got half an hour free if someone will be kind enough to dose me up on intravenous coffee.'

Ella was still standing there admiring the leanly muscled physique so lovingly delineated by the fine fabric of his shirt when Jo leapt to put the kettle on.

'Has Ella told you what we'd planned to do with this lot?' he continued, apparently oblivious to the speculative glance the other staff exchanged. Ella noticed and felt the guilty heat surging up into her cheeks.

Not that she had anything to feel guilty about, unless you counted the way her hormones behaved every time he came into a room, and *that* wasn't something she had any control over.

'You and Ella organised all this?' Serena enquired sweetly, then demanded, 'When? She only started work here yesterday.'

'And yesterday was when Carol dumped that old cardboard box full of the ghosts of Christmas Past on me and told me to decorate the department,' Ella explained swiftly, her brain finally consenting to work. 'Unfortunately, the first person to come within range as I moaned and whinged about it was Mr Gifford.'

'And?' Jo was determined to have her pound of flesh.

'I took one look and suggested that it looked as if the department was long overdue for some new decorations,' Seth butted in, much to her relief. 'Apparently it's the job that's foisted onto the newest members of staff each year and as that's the two of us, we decided to get on with it. Of course, you can help us put them up if you like.'

Everyone seemed to speak at once for a moment, but the general consensus seemed to be that all of them were willing to join in with the decorating detail when there was a brand spanking new selection to play with.

The decorating frenzy went on for most of the afternoon, in between the more urgent job of running a busy hospital department. Everyone seemed to have given a hand at some point, even the patients, and word was spreading to the other neighbouring departments so that they'd had to contend with a growing stream of envious spectators from other wards.

By the time Ella reached the end of her shift she was exhausted but filled with a real sense of satisfaction. Where patients on enforced bed rest had been depressed at the prospect of missing out on the celebrations at home, now the atmosphere in Obs and Gyn was as electric as if it were Christmas Eve already.

There was a marked change in the staff, too. Almost as soon as the first swag was draped over a doorway there had been a new spring in their steps and an almost instant surge of festive camaraderie.

As far as Ella was concerned, it had certainly been the best thing that could have happened at the start of a new job. Not only had she had the chance to meet and work with everyone on duty throughout the whole department, but her introduction had been connected with something that had caused a great deal of pleasure.

At least they all know who I am now, she mused as she donned her scarf and gloves before venturing out into the chilly night. And, in amongst all that, I delivered a perfect set of twins without any need for surgical intervention. A very good day's work if I do say so myself!

'You're looking pleased with yourself!' said a voice in the darkness as she stepped out of the maternity unit door.

'Ooh! You made me jump!' She whirled to face Seth with a shriek. She pressed her hands over her pounding heart, not certain whether it was his unexpected appearance that had caused it to beat so heavily or the sight of his wind-tousled hair and the dark shadow of his emerging beard.

'Sorry about that,' he said with a grimace. 'I've just come out of an interminable meeting and was on my way to my car. When I saw you coming out of the door I realised that I hadn't had a chance to give you a pat on the back for that delivery this afternoon. I was impressed, especially knowing how low the statistics are on a perfectly normal delivery of twins. You managed it beautifully.'

'Thank you,' she said breathlessly, suddenly glowing all over in spite of the vicious little wind whipping round the corner. She hadn't even realised that he'd known about the delivery, let alone that he'd watched it.

Still, she had been rather busy at the time, especially as the second child had been an abnormal presentation that had needed some nifty manoeuvring on her part to facilitate the delivery.

'That was the sort of situation where your neat little hands are much better for the job than mine,' he said generously.

'You mean, all those jokes about gynaecologists being able to decorate their hallway through the front letterbox aren't true?' she teased.

Seth groaned and rolled his eyes. 'You're making me wish I hadn't bothered to stop. If I had a pound for every time I've heard that joke, or one depressingly like it…'

He glanced at his watch and suddenly straightened up as though surprised by what he saw. 'I don't understand where the time goes,' he muttered with a shake of his head. 'I'm going to be late again.'

His farewells were almost absent-minded as he hurried off towards his car and Ella was left with an uncomfortable feeling of *déjà vu*.

'Is he the male version of Cinderella? Will his car turn into a pumpkin if he doesn't lock it in his garage by a certain time?' she muttered as she shivered at the bus stop.

At this time of night she'd deemed it far safer to wait where there was plenty of lighting and within running distance of plenty of help. Walking home through unfamiliar streets was strictly for daylight hours.

'Or perhaps he's a vampire?' she continued under her breath, allowing free rein to her flights of fantasy. 'No. That's wrong. Vampires are supposed to come out at night and sleep by day. Oh, whatever! I just wish I knew where it is that he dashes off to each evening.'

She suddenly noticed that she was getting some very nervous glances from the other people waiting with her at the bus stop and ducked her head to hide behind her upturned collar.

Thinking that habits like talking to herself could get her an extended stay in a room with padded walls if she wasn't careful made her want to giggle, but that probably wasn't a good idea either.

The wretched man was obviously going to send her round the bend at this rate, but it *had* been nice of him to take the trouble to praise her. Not many consultants would have bothered to go out of their way like that—well, they never had before—and it had left her feeling very good about herself and her job.

Now, if only she could get her hormones under control, everything would be perfect. Actually, perfect would be Seth Gifford asking her out for the evening without dashing off somewhere mysterious in the middle of it, but now she was entering the realms of fantasy.

'That dress is perfect,' Carol enthused when she caught sight of Ella at the staff Christmas Ball.

It was one of the hospital's main fundraising functions for the year, and this year the major part of the proceeds were promised to the obs and gyn department for some very high-tech foetal-monitoring gadgetry.

That was probably one of the reasons why so many of the department's staff were attending; that and the fact that Seth had been cornered into promising to dance with all the female members if they paid an appropriate fine into the coffers.

It had started as a joke in the staff lounge, when Donald Crossman had commented wryly that he was glad he and his wife had managed to find a babysitter for the night of the ball.

'Otherwise she'd have made me come by myself to support the cause,' he'd continued. 'And then I'd probably have to spend the entire evening talking to myself—unless I was prepared to make a donation for each woman who was brave enough to dance with me.'

'What a good idea! It sounds as if it would be a very good way of raking in extra donations to boost the funds,' Seth had commented, much to Ella's surprise. He usually spent his time in the staff lounge going over paperwork or catching up on journals rather than joining in with the banter that went on around him. Even now he'd merely lifted his head up long enough to speak and was already turning back to the open file on top of a precarious pile of work he'd brought in with him.

'Wouldn't work in your case, Seth,' Carol pointed out with a suspicious twinkle in her eye, and Ella just knew that she was going to come out with something outrageous. 'We'd have to pay *you* just to get a place on your list!'

That brought his head up with a jerk.

'Oh, but I wasn't intending...' His voice faded when he saw all the expectant faces looking at him and Ella was sure that she saw him swallow before he continued. 'I suppose I ought to show my face at some stage of the evening.'

'Too right!' agreed a bouncy young Australian nurse who had recently joined the department. 'Wouldn't be fair for one of the best-looking single guys not to turn up to take care of all us women wanting to give our money away. I'd put a chunk into the kitty to have a dance.'

In the chorus of agreement and teasing laughter that followed, Ella felt as if she was the only one who had seen Seth wince or noticed the way the colour deepened over the lean planes of his face.

'I very rarely go to functions like this,' he protested weakly, probably already realising that they weren't going to let him win. 'And even when I do, I just do the round of "duty" dances. You know what I mean. Professors' wives and so on. And as I won't be able to be there before nine at the earliest, that wouldn't leave any time for—'

'Poppycock,' Trish retorted brashly as she reached for her purse. 'I'm ready to put my money where my mouth is. How much does everyone think will be a fair amount to contribute to the kitty?'

Seth's eyes were flicking around the room as though he were a cornered animal, and when they met Ella's for just a couple of fraught seconds she almost felt as though he was begging her for help.

What a ridiculous thought. As if someone as good-looking as Seth Gifford would need help in dealing with nubile young women eager to dance with him. As if he would ask *her* for help.

Still the feeling persisted and on an impulse she reached out for the telephone and, under the cover of noisily debating voices, asked for Mr Gifford to be paged, urgently.

She put the phone down and silently started counting. It took seventeen seconds for his pager to shrill its imperative summons and she had to hide her grin when she saw the relief in his eyes as he leapt to his feet and headed across the room to the phone.

She was watching him out of the corner of her eye when he realised what had just happened. The voice on the other end of the phone must have told him that he was ringing from the number that had just paged him because his eyes turned to meet hers as though he knew she was waiting for the connection.

There was a swift flare of surprise in his eyes when he realised what she had done for him and then he put the phone down.

'Sorry. I've got to go,' he said to the room at large without giving any details then glanced back at her. 'Ella, you might be interested in this,' he added vaguely as he turned for the door.

Startled, she leapt to her feet and set off after him, having to scamper to catch up with him.

'Seth?' she called softly, wondering, when he didn't immediately stop to speak to her, whether she'd been wrong about the page. Had it been a genuine call he'd taken instead of hers?

Suddenly he whirled to face her and she nearly cannoned into him.

His eyes were very dark when she looked up into them, their usual silvery grey darkened almost to charcoal and all the more intense for it.

'I don't know why you did it—or even how you knew I needed it—but I just wanted to say thank you for rescuing me,' he said quietly. His voice sounded unusually husky and sent a shiver the whole length of her spine.

Suddenly she was aware of the fact that the two of them were standing in the corridor with their heads together as if they were sharing some kind of illicit rendezvous and the frivolous thought almost made her miss his next words.

'If I can return the favour some time, you only have to ask, Ella.'

She didn't know where the impulse came from…perhaps it was the sincerity in his voice or the fact that she was still fighting her attraction for the man.

Whatever it was, she heard herself saying, 'You could promise me a free dance.'

CHAPTER FOUR

THE ball was being held in one of the larger hotels in the town and the room was already filled with people intent on enjoying themselves.

Sophia would probably have willingly invited her to join the group of staff from the cardiac unit where she worked but Ella had been determined that she was going to mix and mingle with the best of them. This was one of the major social events of the hospital's year and her best chance for meeting members of staff from different departments.

Unfortunately, just the thought of dancing with Seth had been enough to jeopardise all the progress she'd made over the last ten days and she was back to waiting like a giddy teenager for the man to arrive.

She'd actually been able to work side by side with him without a single blush or stammer as long as she didn't think about the promised dance. She'd never admit to a soul that the prospect of being held in his arms had sent her out in search of the perfect dress.

'I love that green,' Jo chimed in, her own sapphire velvet making her long blonde hair look stunning. 'Your eyes look almost the colour of emeralds, and as for that material...it's fabulous.'

Ella had certainly been pleased when she'd seen what the slightly twenties style had done for her. Luckily, at five feet seven inches she was tall enough and slim enough for it to work.

Now all she had to do was wait for her turn to dance with a certain tall, dark handsome man who was entirely too mysterious for her peace of mind.

'Is everyone here?' she asked diffidently, hoping no one could see through her to know what she really wanted to know.

'Apparently, the professor can't make it because one of the twins has come down with chickenpox.'

'Oh, Lord. Can you imagine it?' Trish exclaimed in horror, her dress proudly displaying swirls of the green and gold of her national flag. 'If one of them's got it, it'll spread round all six of them. Nightmare!'

'Is Donald Crossman here yet?' Ella prompted, trying to get the conversation back on her chosen track.

'He certainly is!' Carol exclaimed eagerly. 'He and his wife arrived about ten minutes ago and stopped to say hello. Girls, if you want to see conclusive evidence of exactly how flattering evening dress is, keep an eye out for him. He actually looks quite a bit like Sean Connery playing James Bond.'

'There's no sign of Sexy Seth yet,' Trish announced glumly. 'I've been keeping a special eye out for him to see if I can nab him before he starts wheeling the old chooks around the floor.'

'He did say that he was going to have to arrive late,' Jo reminded her, still chuckling at their Australian colleague's explanation that 'chooks' was Oz for 'chickens'. 'And the ball does go on until midnight, so there's still plenty of time.'

And just you remember it, Ella repeated to herself as she accepted an invitation from one of the paediatric registrars to take to the floor.

Although he was a depressing four years her junior, Martin was a good dancer and an entertaining character with whom she found she had a great deal in common. It wasn't his fault that she felt as if she was just marking time with him until Seth finally arrived to claim her for her promised dance.

Throughout a hectic hour she was on the floor more often than she was off it and had lost count of how many men she'd danced with, but all the while her eyes were straying towards the arched entrance through which Seth would appear.

He still wasn't there when everyone snaked their way past tables groaning with festive fare, and the band was already warming up for the second half of the entertainment when she saw him making his way across the floor.

He looked gorgeous, a fact that Trish had no qualms about announcing to all and sundry, much to the group's hilarity.

If evening dress looked good on middle-aged Donald Crossman, Ella now knew it was positively stunning on Seth. The stark contrast of the black of his suit and hand-tied bow tie against the pure white of his shirt was good enough, but set against the freshly shaved symmetry of an uncompromisingly masculine face it was unforgettable.

Unfortunately, he wasn't making his way towards her, and she had to watch him bow elegantly beside a table of the higher echelon of hospital management.

From a distance Ella thought he was inviting the slightly matronly wife of the chief of surgery to dance and smiled when she saw the woman's startled delight.

She was shocked by the swift stab of jealousy when the woman's rail-thin next-door neighbour simpered up at him and held out a bony claw tipped with blood-red talons.

To her surprise, Seth was shaking his head, reaching instead for the pink-cheeked matron's hand and urging her to join him on the floor.

'Well, that was one in the eye for Mrs Nip-and-tuck,' crowed Carol, letting Ella know that she hadn't been the only one watching that little drama unfold.

'You wouldn't know,' Carol explained in a quiet aside for Ella's and Trish's benefit, 'but she used to be a nurse on the staff here until she married one of the senior plastic surgeons. From the look of her, he's been spending all his time operating on her rather than his patients, and now it looks as if she's on the hunt for fresher meat.'

'Well, all I can say is our Seth is a real gent,' Trish commented supportively. 'Look at the smile on that woman's face. I can almost forgive him for not making a beeline for me. You all know how willing I was to pay for the privilege.'

More and more people had finished eating now, and there was a sudden flurry of activity around the corner of the room their little group had annexed. Ella found herself trying to dance with a whirling dervish—a very energetic trainee male nurse who introduced himself as Vijay and didn't seem to notice that the band was playing a fairly sedate number.

In spite of the fact that the floor was now filled almost beyond capacity, for some reason she still seemed to be able to keep track of Seth's whereabouts.

Regardless of the high proportion of older members of staff, the band had fairly quickly abandoned the slower melodies in favour of more modern ones. The younger element had responded with enthusiasm, rarely dancing with the same partner twice.

Seth was still changing partners with every change of tune but as the evening wore on it began to look as though he'd completely forgotten his promise.

The bandleader had just announced that they were going to be playing the last waltz to bring the night to a close and Ella was on her way to collect her coat when someone caught hold of her elbow and brought her to a halt.

'You can't run off before I can pay my debt,' Seth demanded as he drew her back through the archway.

The lights had been dimmed so that she only had a vague impression of couples swaying together with their arms around each other. Then

Seth drew her towards him, capturing one hand to trap it against his heart while he slid the other around her waist.

Hesitantly, Ella hovered her free hand almost in mid-air, wondering just how 'correctly' Seth expected them to dance together. She'd taken classes for years and could follow almost any partner in any dance, but when it came to putting her hand on Seth, she didn't know what to do.

Then he tightened his hold on her just enough that their bodies fitted together like two halves of a perfect whole and the only logical place to settle it was on his shoulder with her fingers curving along the rich black satin of his collar.

She drew in a steadying breath while she waited for him to take the first step and suddenly recognised the smell of the soap the hospital stocked in the staff showers. Underlying that, though, there was the musky mixture of male skin, and pheromones that belonged exclusively to Seth.

Ella closed her eyes and realised that the two of them were already subconsciously swaying in time to the music, so perfectly in tune with each other that she hadn't realised it was happening. Was this an indication of how well they would move together when they started to dance?

Before they'd had a chance to take a single step together there was a sudden shriek at the other side of the crowd, followed by a cheer that gradually spread out like ripples on a pond.

Ella could have wept with frustration when the band faltered to a halt. How could this be happening when she'd been waiting all evening…all week…to dance with him? It just wasn't fair!

Seth had turned so that they were both facing the little rostrum where the band had been playing all evening and they saw someone beckoning the bandleader down to listen.

'It's like watching a mime performance,' Seth murmured when the bandleader invited the unknown man up onto the rostrum, indicating that he was welcome to use the microphone.

Whatever was happening at the front of the room, no one around Ella and Seth had any idea. The ripples of information hadn't reached that far, but they were surrounded by wild speculation.

'Perhaps someone's had a heart attack,' suggested one.

'Has someone gone into labour?' asked another. 'The wife of one of the charge nurses in A and E looked ready to pop.'

'I bet there's been a punch up,' contended another with unseasonable glee. 'Perhaps someone's drunk too much and propositioned the wrong wife.'

'Inventive lot, aren't they?' Seth said with a chuckle while they waited for the real answer. Ella couldn't find the wit to say anything. She was far too caught up in the wonder of the fact that Seth hadn't loosened his hold on her even though the music had stopped several minutes ago.

Not that she was complaining. She'd never felt so comfortable or so content as she rested her head against his shoulder and waited for events to unfold.

'Hey!' she exclaimed, her attention thoroughly caught when she recognised the young woman now being helped up onto the rostrum to join the little knot of people congregated up there. 'That's my sister, Sophia, getting up onto the stage. What on earth's going on?'

'Your sister works at the hospital, too?'

'Yes. She's a sister in the cardiac department; has been for a couple of years now.' Ella's words were almost automatic. All she was concentrating on was trying to work out what was going on at the front of the room.

'Hello, everybody,' said a gentleman with very distinguished streaks of grey at his temples. He winced when the microphone gave an unearthly shriek. 'I'm sorry to spoil the last few minutes of your evening, especially if you'd just got in the mood for a romantic end to the night.'

There was a chorus of catcalls and cheers at that and he had to hold his hand up for silence.

'The romance has already worked its magic on one couple because the cardiac department is proud to announce a joining of hearts. In spite of all my advice to the contrary, Sophia, here…' he held up her hand '…has just agreed to become engaged to David…'

There was a roar of congratulations as he held up the hand of the man on his other side so Ella probably wasn't the only one who didn't hear his full name.

All she could do was watch as the man who had been making the announcement stepped back and left her sister centre stage with the man she'd apparently just agreed to marry.

'Did you know about this?' Seth demanded over the chaotic noise, his body curved around hers as he leant forward to speak directly into her ear.

Ella shook her head silently, bereft of words. Her eyes were already burning with the threat of tears because she'd known nothing about such a momentous step in her only relative's life. Then she saw the way her sister was looking at the man she'd accepted as her husband-to-be. There was such love in their eyes as they gazed at each other that it almost seemed as if the rest of the world had ceased to exist.

'I don't know anything about him. Not even his name,' she quavered, not even certain that

Seth could hear her. 'Oh, I had a feeling there was someone when I spoke to her the last time, but…well, I haven't seen enough of her since she left home to start her training at eighteen to feel comfortable asking. With five years between us we've never had much in common, even though we both went into medical careers.'

She blinked hard to force the emotional tears back then sniffed, realising too late that if they did start to fall, she'd left her handkerchief in her coat pocket. 'I was hoping that, now we're working at the same hospital, we could at least become friends even if it was too late to ever be confidantes.'

It took Seth's surreptitious donation of a clean white square of fine cotton for her to realise that she'd lost the battle with at least one tear.

'Sorry to turn into a watering can,' she apologised, and blew her nose ferociously. 'I'm happy for her. Really, I am. It's just…' She shrugged, unable to conjure up the words for how she was feeling.

'It must be a bit of a shock to find out something so important in her life at the same time as hundreds of other people,' he suggested compassionately as he led her out of the hall and into the comparative quiet of the corridor. 'But have you thought that she might not have had any option? If the proposal was on the spur of the moment, it could have accidentally been overheard. The news would have spread like wildfire, knowing what that lot are like for gossip. Well, you heard all that speculation going on all around us while we waited for the announcement.'

His suggestion probably made sense but Ella found herself concentrating more on the soothing tone he was using than the words. She certainly hadn't noticed that he'd been leading her towards the concierge so that they could retrieve their coats.

The evening had been full of so many highs and lows that she was more than grateful to let Seth take charge, agreeing meekly when he said he would drop her at her flat.

'This Cinderella didn't get to dance with the handsome prince, but at least she got to ride home in the carriage without it turning into a pumpkin,' she murmured when he drew up outside at the end of a totally silent ride.

'I'm glad I managed to do something right but I'll have to give you an IOU for the dance.'

'No. That's all right. I didn't mean…' she began, stumbling around to find the right words. Not for anything would she have Seth think that she wasn't grateful for the way he'd rescued her when she could have ended up as a soggy puddle of overwrought emotions.

'I insist,' he said quietly, his velvety voice sounding husky in the midnight dark confines of the car.

Subconsciously she noted that vandals must have taken pot-shots at the streetlight again, only days after it had been fixed, but the lack of illumination didn't stop her hearing the sincerity in his voice.

'I always pay my debts,' he insisted, clearly not wanting to let the subject go. 'I promised you a dance and one of these fine days you shall have it. Now, let me escort you to your door before you freeze in that stunning little slip of nothing. Can't have one of our most gifted midwives going down with flu just before Christmas.'

Ella was nearly an hour early and still yawning as she checked her pigeonhole for post in the staff lounge the next morning.

There was a request from the salaries department to confirm one of the digits of her National Insurance number—as soon as possible, please, if she wanted to get her salary paid in before Christmas—and the usual handful of marginally important memos that she glanced through just to make certain that she hadn't missed anything interesting.

She hadn't slept much last night, her mind full of conflicting memories of those few brief moments in Seth's arms before Sophia's bombshell had shattered around her. It was only when she'd concentrated on the care and consideration with which he'd escorted her home that she'd finally been able to doze off, but it hadn't lasted long.

Distracted and overtired, she'd nearly discarded a small plain envelope bearing nothing more than her name before she realised that she wasn't concentrating properly.

'What's this?' she muttered as she fought her way into it impatiently, then stood slack-jawed as she read the contents.

'So that's why I didn't know anything about it,' she whispered as tears prickled her eyes again. The words swam over the paper but she hardly needed to see them to know what they said.

'Little Sister Gabby,' it began, bringing back memories of teasing exchanges over the comparative lengths of their names. 'I've got an announcement to make and if I wait until I can see you face to face it will be too late,' she'd continued in handwriting atrocious enough to qualify her as a doctor.

'I'm engaged!

We didn't want to spoil the surprise as we've kept it a secret from everyone else at the hospital, but I couldn't let you find out in front of all those people as if you didn't mean any more to me than they did...' Sophia had written in her usual exuberant way.

'We're getting married in March and you've just *got* to be my bridesmaid. Oh, Gabby, I'm just so happy. See you tonight after the announcement and I'll tell you all about it…all about *him*. Love, Big Sister Soph.'

'Problem?' murmured an achingly familiar voice right behind her and suddenly the moment became perfect.

'No. Yes. Oh, not really,' she sniffed and brushed a couple of stray tears away with her fingertips. 'Here. Read this. It proves that you were right…more or less.'

She passed Seth the letter and watched while he skimmed the contents with practised speed.

'If only you'd thought to check your pigeonhole yesterday before you went home…' he said ruefully as he handed it back to her.

'Oh, Lord! I'll have to phone her to let her know why I didn't speak to her after the ball,' Ella exclaimed. She glanced around, trying to remember where to find the closest pay phone. 'What must she have thought when I just disappeared?'

'Sorry, but I'm afraid it'll have to wait a bit longer,' he said as he grabbed the edge of her sleeve to stop her moving away. 'That's why I came looking for you. Carol needs some help. She's one midwife down through sickness this morning and one delayed in traffic and she's got two mums coming to the boil. She was hoping you'd be early and sent me to see if you'd arrived yet.'

Instantly, duty took precedence, the letter unceremoniously thrust into the pocket of her drawstring cotton trousers as she gathered her thoughts.

'Which room is she in and where does she want me?' she said briskly, already in motion towards the door as she began to pepper him with questions. 'Do you know if there are any complications expected with either delivery? Are they both full term?'

'I don't know much more than I've told you,' he said with both hands held up defensively. 'I'm just the messenger. Carol will have to give you the low-down. Don't forget,' he called after her as she set off towards the delivery suites, 'you can call me if you need an extra pair of hands. I'm not due in surgery till nine and I don't mind an excuse to get away from paperwork.'

Ella threw a brief word of thanks over her shoulder as she disappeared around the first corner.

'Ella! Thank goodness you're here!' Carol exclaimed, beckoning frantically. 'I'm not nearly schizophrenic enough to deal with two patients at once, not on opposite sides of the corridor.'

'What have you got and which one do you want me to take?' Ella didn't waste time. Seeing Carol in such a state was so unusual that she knew things were desperate.

'I've got one of "my" first-time mums in here in transition with a husband who looks as if he's about to keel over any second.'

She broke off for a moment when her patient shouted something extremely uncomplimentary about her less-than-helpful spouse and informed him in no uncertain terms that if he wanted any more children he could give birth to them himself.

'That's transition,' Ella said and they grinned at each other before Carol continued.

'In there…' she pointed to the delivery suite on the opposite side of the corridor '…is a young woman called Virginia Drew who walked in off the street about twenty minutes ago in active labour. We have no medical records but she says she's full term. She's complaining of headache and her blood pressure is rather lower than I'd like. On the good side, the baby's head seems to be perfectly positioned for a straightforward delivery and Mum seems to be otherwise fit and healthy.'

'OK, Carol.' Ella gave a mock salute. 'Best of luck in there.'

'It sounds like I'm going to need it if she doesn't get to second stage fairly quickly. Still, her choice of vocabulary is probably concentrating the father's mind wonderfully.'

Ella was still smiling when she entered the delivery suite on the opposite side of the corridor but one look at her patient's grey sweaty face had her hurrying to her bedside.

'Virginia, how are you feeling?' she asked, her eyes already flying over the displays on the continuous monitor. Tachycardia and her blood pressure was much too low for a woman in normal labour.

'I feel…dreadful,' she muttered, each word seeming to take a monumental effort. 'Weak. Dizzy. Thirsty. My head…my back…my belly…' Her hand hovered protectively over the taut mound covered only by the brightly patterned gown and the wide band that held the foetal monitor in position.

Ella placed her hand over the baby and her heart gave a sickening jolt when she saw the monitor warning that it was becoming distressed.

'Are you having a contraction?' she demanded, only realising how sharp her voice was when Virginia looked startled.

'No.' She shook her head weakly, and when she winced Ella realised it must have jarred her aching head. 'But…it will come. Another one…always comes.'

Except that the belly under Ella's hand was absolutely rigid, and it shouldn't have been unless Virginia's uterus was contracting.

A swift apology was all Ella had time for before she flipped the hem of the gown up.

'No blood,' she breathed, half in relief and half in terror, while her own heart rate doubled. All the factors for a differential diagnosis were whirling round in her brain but she kept coming up with disaster.

She was praying as she reached for the phone to page Seth. Oh, please, God, don't let it be an abrupted placenta.

She'd never even seen one before but she knew that there wasn't a second to waste. If the placenta *had* torn away from the wall of the uterus her patient could be bleeding to death inside without a drop of blood to show it. And without that vital blood supply, the baby would die within minutes.

'Carol!' she called urgently, pushing the door to the delivery suite open with her shoulder while she tore open the packaging on a giving set. 'What fluids have you got in there? I need them, *now*!'

One small part of her brain registered the astonishing fact that her hands were perfectly steady as they slid the wide-bore needle into position and set the saline running wide open.

'Virginia? Can you hear me?' she called as she pulled all of the pillows out from under Virginia's head, settled the mask tightly in position over her face and turned up the oxygen volume being delivered through it. The monitors showed that she still had a pulse, but her blood pressure was plummeting. Her patient was frighteningly quiet, her eyelids barely fluttering in response to Ella's voice or her touch.

On the way past the bottom of the bed she piled the pillows under the flaccid legs, hoping to drain at least some of the blood they contained up towards her heart so that it could be pumped up to keep her brain alive.

The phone shrilled just as Carol shouldered her way through the door with several bags of fluids.

'My God! What's happened?' she demanded as she reached automatically for the phone.

'That's Seth, I hope. Tell him I think it's an abrupted placenta. She's in shock and needs an immediate Caesarean or we're going to lose both of them. Should we transfer her up to Theatre?' Her hands were working even faster than her mouth, inserting a second IV into the other arm and setting it going as fast as possible to deliver fluid into the woman's veins. If the fluid volume dropped too far the heart would simply stop beating.

'He's on his way now,' Carol said as she hung the extra fluids on the IV stands and automatically reached for another giving set to connect to veins in her legs before they had a chance to collapse completely. 'He's bringing the anaesthetist with him so they can assess her and operate here. This is Hartmann's solution going in.'

So they can operate here… Hearing her colleague's positive slant on what was about to happen, Ella smiled bleakly, knowing that even with an IV running into each of her limbs, their patient could be losing blood volume faster than they could replace it. In that situation it would just be a matter of time before her brain shut down for ever, making any operation useless.

In the meantime, if she was interpreting the readings on the monitor correctly, that little baby was trapped inside his mother's body and was already slowly being starved of the oxygen he needed to survive.

There was a sudden bang at the other end of the department as though a door had been flung open in a hurry and had hit the wall. Ella's head shot up when the unexpected noise was followed by the sound of running feet.

By the time Seth reached the room Carol was waiting for him by the door, holding a disposable plastic gown out for him, swiftly followed by gloves and a mask.

'How long has she been like this?' he demanded as his eyes flew from the readings on the monitors to the ominously still figure.

'Sudden onset,' Ella said briskly as she stripped the gown out of his way. 'Came in about half an hour ago with slightly low blood pressure that suddenly started to drop without visible blood loss. Tachycardic, dizzy and sweating then loss of consciousness.'

Ella would never forget the next few minutes as long as she lived.

She never would have believed that anyone could move so fast to prepare a patient for major surgery. Seth wasn't even working in an operating theatre and she was sure he didn't have half the supplies he needed but it didn't appear to slow him down at all.

It seemed just seconds later that his incision into the uterus released a shocking flood of dark red blood and then he was reaching a gloved hand in through the incision to find the child.

'Oh, God, please,' she whispered when he withdrew a blood-coated scrap that dangled limply in mid-air.'

'Where's that paediatrician?' he demanded as Ella leapt to take the child from him, supporting the weight of the tiny body while he swiftly clipped and cut the cord. 'He should be here by now…' he continued impatiently, only to fall silent at the sound of another set of running feet.

'Don't resuscitate,' the panting man said as soon as he caught sight of the child, his hands full of a selection of sterile packages. 'I'll intubate immediately. He'll need pulmonary lavage to get all that muck out of his lungs.'

As he was speaking he was already directing Ella to position the child but a clock was ticking away inside her head, counting off the seconds that the tiny infant had gone without taking that first important measure of oxygen.

There was a clatter outside the door and another influx of people arrived, wheeling a humidicrib with its own power supply and another pile of specialised sterile packages.

Ella relinquished the fragile body into their care, able only to watch while they worked to try to ameliorate the effects of his traumatic arrival in the world.

'How is he?' Seth demanded suddenly, his head bent over his own task as he added bleakly, 'Please, get him going because I don't know whether his mother will ever be able to have another one.'

Ella could only imagine what damage he had found inside the uterus and would have to wait until later to ask what he'd been able to do about it.

She glanced around the room, looking for Carol, only to realise that her colleague must have returned to her own patient at some stage. So much had happened in such a short space of time that she'd completely lost track.

As if on cue, there was the sound of an indignant cry from the room on the other side of the corridor and Ella's heart ached to hear the same sound from *her* little charge.

Not that he would be able to make a sound with a tube down his throat, even if he had the breath to do it.

The busy staff clustered around the humidicrib seemed to have been working on him for ever but as she couldn't see what they were doing she could only guess. She only knew that they must have been connecting the various sensors positioned on his body to the monitors because suddenly there was the sharp sound of a little ragged heartbeat.

There was a muted cheer and a definite air of relief that at least one of their patients seemed to be winning the battle.

'I think we've just about got him stable enough to get him out of your way,' the paediatrician announced, his protective clothing covered with blood as if he'd been slaughtering the child rather than trying to save his life. 'He'll be in ICU for the foreseeable future—at least until we find out if his lungs have been damaged.'

He followed his team out of the room, pausing briefly in the doorway to catch Ella's eye with a concerned expression in his own and nod towards the frantic activity still going on over the baby's mother. 'You will let me know?'

CHAPTER FIVE

'SHALL I phone ICU, or will you?' Ella asked Seth over her shoulder. 'Mr Tufnell wanted to know how you got on with his charge's mum.'

She was pretending to concentrate on stirring the last soggy teabag around in one mug before scooping it out and repeating the process in another. In reality she was still trying to get her scrambled emotions under control.

'I dropped in on my way back from delivering Virginia,' Seth informed her with a quiet air of satisfaction and a word of thanks for the steaming mug she handed him.

Ella couldn't bring herself to meet his eyes yet. Her emotions were still too close to the surface and she didn't want to make a complete fool of herself. In the last few weeks she'd discovered that he had that effect on her, as if she'd lost the ability to hide what she was feeling.

'Baby Drew is holding his own so far and Tufnell doesn't think there's been too much lung damage,' Seth continued. 'When they did the lavage there was very little muck in there. He's more concerned about possible brain damage because we don't know what degree of oxygen deprivation he'd suffered before we got to him.'

'And it could be a while before that becomes evident, even if his brain scans don't look too bad,' she finished for him.

'At least once I got Virginia suctioned out I was able to see that the placenta hadn't become completely detached, but how much use his body was able to make of what was left…' He left the thought unfinished.

Ella stared into the mug cradled between her palms as though the answer to the world's oldest riddle was hidden there.

'Seth,' she heard herself say in a voice made shaky by a dangerous overload of emotion, 'I just wanted to tell you how…how impressed I was by what you did today.' She had to swallow before she could continue. 'When you did the incision and all that blood came pouring out…' She shook her head, unable to go on.

'I think that was the scariest thing I've ever done,' he admitted quietly, and the sincerity in his voice drew her eyes to him the way nothing else could. 'At that moment I really thought that there was no hope of being able to save either of them, but I was damned if I was going to give up without giving it a try.'

He ran his fingers roughly through his hair and Ella was almost certain that she saw them tremble slightly.

'Well, I've certainly never seen a Caesarean performed that fast before.' She couldn't help it if he heard the awe in her voice. There was so much in the world of medicine that impressed her, but after this, Seth was in a class of his own. 'And you weren't even in a proper theatre when you did it.'

'It was a team effort,' he said uncomfortably, but she could tell from the heightened colour along his cheekbones that her words had meant something to him. 'I couldn't have done it without Pali taking care of the anaesthesia, and the scrub nurse sorting out the nearest equivalent to the equipment I needed.

'As for you…' he continued in a gravelly voice. 'None of us would have had a chance of making a difference if you hadn't kept your head and kept her going until we could get to her. If you hadn't got those fluids up and running when you did, neither mum nor baby would have stood a chance. And as for tilting her that way…that actually caused the baby to press the placenta against the area of greatest blood loss and slowed it down.'

The admiration in his words and in his eyes was the final straw. Her composure crumpled without a second's warning and the tears started to pour out of her.

'Oh, Seth, I was so scared,' she sobbed, desperately embarrassed to have lost control in front of him but helpless to stop. 'When I realised what was happening, and that she could die right there in front of me if I didn't do the right thing…'

Suddenly he was there beside her and she was wrapped in his arms, strong and all-encompassing, and he was murmuring supportively in her ear.

'But your instincts were absolutely spot on. You called for help, you cleared her airway and started pumping the oxygen in and you supported her circulation with a forest of drips. I can't think of anything more that you could have done in such a short space of time.'

'But—'

'You even managed to light a firecracker under the right people to get some blood delivered at the double. Everything I needed, you seemed to have worked out in advance so that it was ready and waiting for me. I promise you, my little team was well impressed with your unflappability, and it takes a lot to impress them.'

His deep husky voice was definitely having a calming effect on her and as his words gradually sank in she was able to admit to her darker thoughts.

'It's just… Oh, Seth, I just feel so guilty that she nearly died when I was supposed to be taking care of her.'

'No, Ella. Don't you *dare* go beating yourself up like that,' he said sternly, giving her a shake to emphasise his words. 'You walked into an ongoing situation without any warning except a note that her blood pressure was slightly low, and you coped brilliantly. Instead of feeling guilty you should be over the moon that it looks as if both of them are going to make it, in large measure because of your quick thinking.'

Ella drew in a deep shuddering breath and held it for a moment before releasing it in a steady stream, trying to get rid of her churning emotions along with it.

'Feeling better?' he prompted, loosening his hold on her just enough to look down at her face.

'Mmm-hmm.' She nodded, feeling a blush work its way up her cheeks when she realised exactly how closely he'd been holding her.

'In that case,' he said, something different in the expression in his eyes telling her that the mood had changed completely, 'please, may I get up from the floor before my knees are crippled for ever?'

'Your knees?' she repeated with a blink, only then realising that he'd actually been kneeling on the hard floor beside her chair to comfort her.

She laughed. It was watery, but a definite improvement on the last few minutes.

'Perhaps you *had* better get up or someone will walk in and get the wrong impression,' she joked unevenly. 'They might think there's going to be a second wedding in the Buchan family.'

'Me and my big mouth,' Ella muttered hours later as she relived the uncomfortable silence that had suddenly descended over them after her teasing comment.

Until she'd heard the words coming out of her own mouth she hadn't realised just how far down the road of attraction her subconscious had gone. Until that moment, she hadn't realised that she'd gone way beyond a simple appreciation of Seth as a sexy man who'd set her hormones in an uproar the first time she'd seen him.

Her cheeks were flaming again as she pulled the covers up over her head, remembering the utter shock on his face as her words had registered.

It was embarrassingly obvious that he didn't see her in the same way at all.

'So, having put my foot in my mouth, how am I supposed to face him tomorrow and the day after that?' she groaned. 'Do I bite the bullet and apologise, or pretend that it never happened?'

At least the next day was Christmas Eve, with all its attendant jollity. Perhaps there would be too much going on for the two of them to be alone. Then, with any luck, he'd have time to forget all about it.

In the meantime, as far as she knew, no one had ever died of embarrassment…even if they'd wished they could.

'This is a madhouse,' Carol complained over the sound of Christmas carols coming from the nearest four-bedded room.

'You're only moaning because someone spilled the beans about today being your birthday,' Jo said smugly. 'As if your name wasn't a big enough clue.'

'I wouldn't mind if that was *all* they'd done,' Carol countered grimly, glaring at all three of them. 'It was the fact that they've announced to all and sundry that it's my *thirtieth* birthday that hurts.'

'Well, it seems to have got you the sympathy vote if that pile of parcels is anything to go by,' Serena said with a slightly envious glance at the stack of intriguingly wrapped gifts under a brightly coloured banner proclaiming the fact that Carol was now Flirty Thirty.

'Knowing my luck, it's probably all the constituent parts for my very own Zimmer frame,' she predicted glumly. 'Or perhaps everyone pushed the boat out and contributed towards a stair lift in case I can't manage to walk up to my flat any more.'

'Huh,' Ella scoffed as she looked at the slim woman who looked elegant even in theatre pyjamas. 'You're one of those people who'll be fit enough to take up hang-gliding when you're eighty, then pushing the rest of us around in our bath chairs.'

Carol laughed and then shrugged. 'What can I tell you? I just happen to have inherited great genes that make us look younger than we are. And it would have worked, too. I could have been twenty-nine for years yet, if someone hadn't done the dirty. Wait till I find out who it was. They won't get a weekend off duty until they're retirement age.'

They were all laughing as they separated to go to their individual tasks.

Because it was Christmas Eve there were no surgical cases scheduled, and most of the patients still recovering from previous lists would be going home today. But that didn't mean that an emergency of some sort couldn't land on their doorstep at any moment.

It also didn't mean that babies were deciding to wait until after the holiday to be born. They'd had one delivery in the early hours of the morning—a beautiful little full-term baby girl with a head full of thick dark hair. Then, just a few minutes ago, another of the patients who'd been attending the hospital's antenatal clinic had rung to say that she thought she was in labour and was on her way in.

'Poor Mrs Hockney. She's had a couple of false alarms already,' Jo had said when Carol had told them about the call. 'I was beginning to worry that she might leave it too late when the *real* event started just because she didn't want to "waste our time" again.'

'I don't think her husband would let that happen. He'd be too scared that he was going to have to deliver the baby himself. He was one of our tough-guy fathers who faint when they see the "this is how your baby comes into the world" video.'

Ella chuckled wryly. 'There's usually one in every antenatal group, flexing his muscles as though getting his wife pregnant was something only the physically perfect can do.'

'They're usually the ones to fold first,' Carol agreed. 'It's the quiet, slightly nervous ones who most often get so involved in the whole process that they surprise themselves by coping with it. You just have to make sure they've got a chair to sit on when their knees go wobbly and remind them to hold their wife's hand.'

The advice came back to Ella later that morning when Peter Hockney suddenly slid down the wall and ended up sitting on the floor with a dazed expression on his face.

'At least he didn't hit his head,' his wife said in a resigned voice as she watched the junior sister check him over before returning to her post at the other side of the bed. 'He'd never live it down at work if he went in to tell them the baby's been born and had to display a face full of stitches.'

The last words were forced out between gritted teeth as the next big contraction took hold, and then she began to concentrate, totally giving herself over to doing the breathing exercises she'd been taught at the department's antenatal classes.

The rest of her labour was relatively quick and uneventful with each of them casting occasional glances at the green-faced figure now huddled on a chair well out of sight of anything remotely gory.

It was the conspiratorial grins that the three women shared that he should have taken note of, even if he couldn't hear what they were saying.

'If he thinks that his squeamishness is going to get him out of changing the baby's nappy, he's got another think coming,' Christine murmured in the brief respite before the next contraction, her Northern roots suddenly very evident in her accent. 'I don't believe that the men should have all the pleasure of having children while the women do all the hard work, and that goes for after they're born as well as putting them there!'

Ella was still chuckling quietly as she carefully controlled the head as it passed through the perineum.

'Keep panting for me, Christine,' she directed quickly. 'The head's out and I'm just going to feel around the baby's neck to check that the cord isn't in the way, so don't push for a second.'

'Well, hurry up!' she gasped before panting furiously.

'All clear! You can push as soon as you like,' Ella said and concentrated on delivering first one then the other shoulder.

'It's a girl!' she announced as the rest of the baby slithered out into her waiting hands in a rush. 'It's a girl and she's beautiful. Looks just like her mum.'

There was a sudden indignant cry and all four little limbs began to flail the air as Ella held the tiny being up for the new mother to see.

There was a groan and a thud in the corner and they all glanced across to see that one new father was now lying stretched out on the floor, unconscious.

'You wait until you're old enough to understand this story,' Christine confided to the naked little body sprawled across her chest while Kerry checked her Apgar score.

She stroked a gentle finger over her new daughter's damp hair and grinned up at Ella and Kerry. 'This is one girl who won't be buying into the "big strong man" myth.'

'Don't be too hard on us,' said a voice from the doorway and Ella's heart leapt into her throat.

'Christine, this is Mr Gifford, one of the consultants,' she said, hoping she sounded calmer than she felt while she waited for him to announce the reason for his visit. In the meantime she busied herself with checking the baby over while she wrapped her in a warmed blanket.

'I hope you don't mind,' Seth said, speaking directly to her patient. 'But I heard your daughter's cry and couldn't keep from sticking my head round the door.' He leant closer as if to whisper confidentially. 'I've always found new babies totally irresistible. Is she your first?'

He was standing right beside the bed now, his eyes flicking from the swaddled bundle cradled in her mother's arms to Ella as she watched the byplay in amusement.

To pretend that his love of their tiny babies was a secret was nonsense. All the midwives knew his weakness—that he couldn't wait to get his hands on them.

'She's our first and our last, unless my husband can get his act together,' she muttered darkly, then screwed her face up in discomfort. 'Ow! I'm having contractions again. It's not twins, is it?'

'No such luck,' Ella teased as Seth took his chance at getting his hands on the baby while she bent over the business end of things. 'You'll have to go through the whole nine months again if you want another one. This is just the afterbirth.'

'Hey…' said a groggy voice at floor level. 'Is that my baby?'

'It certainly is,' Seth confirmed cheerfully, carrying the little bundle across and offering a helping hand to the struggling figure. 'Are you ready for a proper introduction?'

'I would be if I didn't keep going light-headed,' he mumbled as he slumped on the chair again. 'I don't know what's the matter with me.'

'I bet you forgot to have anything to eat before we left the house,' his wife said suddenly. 'You've been like this before when you're changing shifts, just because you don't feel like having your dinner when it feels as if it ought to be breakfast time.'

'If it's just low blood sugar, I could probably find a cup of sweet tea to tide you over,'

Kerry offered, then turned to Christine. 'I could make that tea for two, if you like?'

'Oh, yes, please,' the young woman said fervently. 'I could murder a cup!'

'Well, by the time it arrives, we should be all tidied up here,' Ella said as she started whisking the less aesthetic aftermath of a birth out of sight. She would give Peter Hockney the benefit of the doubt that he'd only passed out because he'd forgotten to eat, but there was no point in tempting fate if it had really been squeamishness.

'Meantime, don't bother hurrying, because I get the best job of all,' Seth murmured, totally absorbed as he ran a gentle finger down a petal-soft cheek.

For a moment Ella stood mesmerised by the picture the two of them made, the tall, utterly masculine man cradling the tiny child so protectively in his arms.

In a sudden flash of madness she could imagine that it was their child that he was holding, and there was a deep ache of unexpected longing inside her.

* * *

'Right, Ella,' Carol said briskly. 'I've got it all arranged. There's punch and mince pies in the staff lounge in fifteen minutes. Can you pass the message around?'

'Good timing. You'll catch two shifts that way, one as they're going off and the other coming on,' Ella said with a smile. 'I'll do a quick whisk around and see who I can find. I take it you're intending this to include the whole department?'

'And any extra stragglers like SCBU and Paediatrics who happen to be around at the right moment,' she said generously. 'It's Christmas Eve, so the more the merrier. There'll even be crackers to pull and the wearing of silly paper hats will be obligatory.'

'We get plenty of practice at that with those dreadful disposable knickers we have to wear on our heads,' Ella grumbled as she set off to spread the word. 'Still, if we're all wearing them it isn't so bad.'

She was pleasantly surprised by everyone's reaction to the invitation, having had nothing like it at her previous hospital.

'Of course we're coming,' Jo said, speaking for Serena. 'Wouldn't miss it. Carol really sets the holiday off with a sparkle; puts us all in the right mood.'

'I'd be delighted to come,' Donald Crossman said with a beam. 'I've been hovering around the department for the last half-hour just waiting to find out if Carol was doing it again. This year, though,' he confided in a low voice, tapping his pocket significantly, 'we've arranged a little surprise for her, as it's a milestone birthday. I shall drag Seth along, too. He hasn't been here long enough to know about Carol's little get-together.'

Just the sound of his name and the thought that he would be joining them for a social occasion was enough to put an extra spring in Ella's step.

It was no one's business but hers that she'd stopped off in the cloakroom to brush her hair until it gleamed and had freshened her make-up, and she was in the mood to enjoy herself when she and Kerry made their way to the staff lounge at the appointed time.

'Wow, look at this!' she exclaimed to Kerry when she saw the number of people already there. 'Is there anybody left to run the department?'

'Luckily, there isn't anything much going on at the moment,' she pointed out seriously. 'Nobody in labour—so far—nobody recovering from surgical anaesthetic, and everybody else knows that they only have to press their bell to have one of us on the way at the trot.'

'In the meantime, let's get our hands on some of that food. I'm starving!' Ella exclaimed, impressed by the variety on offer. It certainly wasn't anything as tame as she'd been expecting.

'It's an alcohol-free punch so we don't end up as a Christmas statistic, but all the food is wonderful,' Jo pointed out as she joined them at the tables pushed together at one side of the room. They were almost groaning under the weight of savouries and sweets.

There was the sudden sound of something being tapped against a glass and the chatter subsided enough for Donald Crossman to make himself heard.

'This is probably the best moment to speak, while the rest of you have something in your mouths so you can't heckle and before someone's pager goes off,' he began, to a round of laughter. 'Now, Carol, on behalf of all your guests, I would like to thank you for your hospitality again this year. I believe this is the third time you've organised it and long may the tradition continue. I firmly believe that it is good for morale within the department.

'The only problem is,' he continued with a mock scowl at some of the extra bodies that Ella didn't recognise as members of the department, 'it could get so popular that we'd need to transfer it to a large marquee on the lawn to accommodate the numbers. Then we'd probably have to move the date to some time with warmer weather and before you knew it, instead of being our department's private Christmas get-together, it would end up the Hospital Summer Ball.'

'He's a good speaker for all that he seems so quiet and shy,' Kerry murmured under the cover of everyone's laughter. 'Not at all pompous and overbearing, like some consultants.'

'However,' he continued, reaching into the inside pocket of his suit jacket with one hand while he gestured towards the incriminating banner with the other, 'as we all know, today is also your birthday, and this year it's one of those special ones that deserve special recognition.'

He drew out an envelope and presented it to a scarlet-faced Carol to the accompaniment of whoops and cheers.

Carol's words were inaudible to the group over by the table but the expression on her face as she protestingly opened the envelope was something else. She seemed utterly amazed.

So many people were calling out to find out what it was that Donald tapped his glass again.

'For the nosier element among us, it's a voucher for a weekend for two at a central London hotel with tickets to the show of her choice—how we discovered that information is classified. And,' he added over a renewed round of laughter and applause, 'it's not just for her birthday but also in recognition of the wonderful way she runs her ward and everyone in it.'

'Excuse me,' said a voice behind Ella, and she whirled to face Seth standing just inside the doorway in the only clear space. She'd been wondering where he was, but she certainly hadn't expected him to arrive carrying a cake with thirty glowing candles on it.

Donald must have been looking out for him because the glass was chimed again.

'If everyone would like to clear a path,' he requested, obviously starting to enjoy his role as master of ceremonies, 'we'd like Carol to have a chance to blow out the candles before the intense heat sets the fire alarms off!'

Everyone joined in the birthday song then a chorus of 'We wish you a merry Christmas' before they got down to the real business of eating and chatting.

After the brief flare of excitement, Ella found that she wasn't really enjoying herself. It was too much of a reminder of everything that was missing from her life.

Ever since she and Sophia had lost their parents in a skiing accident in their mother's native Italy, Christmas just hadn't been the same and birthdays had been all but forgotten.

As often as not she'd volunteered to be on duty over the festive season so that staff with families could share the day with them. This year, now that they were actually working in the same hospital for the first time, she'd actually thought that she and Sophia might have got together. Her sister's recent engagement would have put paid to that idea. Sophia was probably going to be spending it with David and her future in-laws while they planned the wedding.

Appetite gone, she slipped unobtrusively out of the room and took a silent wander through the department.

There was laughter and conversation all around her with knots of visitors at almost every bed, and if there were more than the regulation number here and there, well, it *was* Christmas Eve after all.

She watched from the shadowed side of the corridor while Peter Hockney cradled his tiny daughter. She had a feeling that he was going to turn out to be a far more adaptable daddy than Christine had feared. Who knew, perhaps they'd even get him changing nappies before he took the two of them home tomorrow.

Tomorrow. Christmas Day, with Christine and her new daughter being welcomed into Peter's family home, the living proof that their genetic line was continuing into the next generation.

And what would she be doing tomorrow? Not even eating unless she got herself moving before all the shops closed.

Ella took a quick glance at her watch and realised that she should have left nearly an hour ago…not that she begrudged Carol the extra time for their little department get-together.

She was still smiling at Carol's almost incoherent thanks for the surprises the department had sprung on her when she turned on her heel and ploughed straight into Seth.

'Careful!' He caught her by the elbow to steady her, his hand very warm on the skin bared by the short sleeve of her scrubs as it lingered just a fraction too long for her peace of mind.

'Sorry. I was just going to get my coat and—'

'Hey! Have you seen what you're standing under?' called a teasing voice from the little four-bedded bay, his attention probably caught by her exclamation of surprise.

They both glanced up to see a sprig of green leaves and white berries that someone had added to their decorations.

'It's mistletoe, and you're not supposed to stand there looking at it,' joked Peter Hockney. 'You're supposed to take advantage of it.'

Ella's face flamed but she couldn't drag her eyes away from the soft grey of Seth's. In all the weeks they'd been working together he could probably have stolen a kiss if he'd been interested. She certainly wouldn't have stopped him, not if she was ever going to find out if her dreams could possibly be as good as reality.

Now here they were awkwardly trapped into a situation that had few easy exits, especially with the Hockneys looking on so expectantly.

If either she or Seth were to object to such an innocuous Christmas ritual it would seem…

'Merry Christmas, Ella,' Seth murmured softly as he placed his hands on her shoulders and angled his head towards her, taking her completely by surprise as he brushed his lips gently over hers.

CHAPTER SIX

SHOCK made Ella gasp, opening her lips under Seth's so that she could suddenly taste the sharp tang of the punch he'd been drinking.

Almost as though he was reacting to the innocent invitation of her open mouth, his hands tightened on her shoulders, drawing her closer for a second touch that quickly escalated out of hand.

His mouth was soft and persuasive but his tongue was wicked, setting off jagged bolts of lightning that struck deep inside her, robbing her of breath.

Her knees refused to lock any more, leaving her leaning weakly against him and clinging to the solid width of his shoulders as she tentatively touched her tongue to his.

He groaned, the husky sound tightening nerves right in the pit of her stomach as he tilted his head still further then began to explore the dark secrets of her mouth.

'Whooee!' Peter Hockney crowed, shocking the two of them into an instant and embarrassing realisation of where they were and what they were doing. 'He might be slow on the uptake, but, boy...!'

Seth wrenched his mouth away from hers, grasping her shoulders to push her away while he stared into her eyes with a look of...of horror.

Out of the corner of her eye Ella saw the swift jab Christine aimed at her gleeful husband's ribs.

'You want to be careful,' the young woman said knowingly with a glance at her new baby. 'The two of you ought to know better than most what that sort of thing can lead to.'

Without a word, Ella and Seth turned and made their way out of the ward, with every hurried step having to listen to the chuckles they were leaving behind.

'That will probably be all over the hospital by the time we can get our coats on,' Seth grated, barely glancing in her direction as though he couldn't bear to look at her.

'I doubt that we'll be the only members of staff to have had a kiss under the mistletoe,' she retorted sharply. She was hurt that he seemed to see their kiss as something wrong, something distasteful, while she…

Never in her life had she had a kiss that had short-circuited every synapse in her brain. Never had the simple contact between two mouths felt so utterly right that she'd never wanted it to end.

And all he could think about was that people might gossip about it—as if that was all that mattered.

As if by unspoken agreement they paused outside the door to the staff lounge. Somehow the sound of all those cheerful voices and all that happy laughter was more than she could deal with at the moment and she was just about to take her leave when he spoke.

'I'm sorry, Ella,' he said gruffly, still unable to meet her eyes. 'That shouldn't have happened.'

Stung, she retorted before she could get her brain into proper working order.

'Don't worry about it,' she said with a shaky attempt at indifference. 'It was just a mistletoe kiss—par for the course at this time of year.'

'Except it took place in front of patients and it got out of hand,' he said heavily. 'It was… It was unprofessional and I apologise.'

With those words he finally managed to force himself to meet her eyes and she could have cried when she saw the expression in them.

In view of his words, she'd expected that he would look unhappy, but she hadn't expected to see such overwhelming guilt.

'I'll survive,' she promised light-heartedly as she turned away from him, but inside she wasn't absolutely sure that she would. At this precise moment she wasn't certain that anything in her life was going to be the same ever again.

She heard him mutter something behind her and for just a moment it sounded as if he'd said, 'I'm not sure I will.' But she must have been mistaken, because when she turned back he was already disappearing around the corner in the corridor.

*   *   *

Angry and disappointed, Ella dumped the rest of the uneaten pizza in the bin and made her way to the bathroom to brush her teeth.

The miserable face looking back at her in the mirror went part way to bringing her back to her senses. So what if she'd paid a silly amount to have blonde highlights put in her hair to mimic the effects of sunlight on the dark auburn strands. And she might as well not have bothered with freshening up her make-up for all the good it had done her.

'If you looked like that when he kissed you, then it's no wonder that he didn't want to do it again,' she said, deliberately pulling an ugly face at herself. 'And it's understandable that a consultant might be worried about the proprieties, especially if we'd gone any further…'

Gone any further? She couldn't help a huff of disbelieving laughter when she remembered just how close she'd come to spontaneous combustion—and there hadn't been a thought in her head about stopping him…*them*. Never before had she felt one tenth…one hundredth…one millionth of what she'd felt when Seth had kissed her.

Before, even in the midst of an embrace, she'd always had to think about what response she should make to what was happening to her—whether she should put her arms around the man, whether she should open her mouth when he kissed her.

With Seth, for the first time in her life it had just *happened*, unleashed by that first heated glance.

It was only now that she was thinking about it that she remembered instinctively wrapping her arms around his shoulders so that their bodies had met like two halves of a perfect whole. Only after it was all over did she remember the way their lips had met and their tongues had duelled in the dark secrecy of their mouths, giving and taking in perfect mimicry of the seamless way their bodies would have joined.

'And he said it shouldn't have happened,' she whispered into her pillow as the first tear trickled down the side of her nose. 'It was the most perfect moment of my life and he…he apologised for it.'

* * *

'Happy Christmas, Gabriella,' she said sadly the next morning as she opened the solitary present—a brightly wrapped gift from Sophia that she'd found tucked into her pigeonhole—and which she'd carried home from the hospital last night.

A negligee set, in a shade of green so dark that in the folds it seemed to be black, slithered out of the nest of tissue paper onto her lap. She held it up to admire it, knowing that it was the perfect choice against her pale skin and auburn hair.

It was pure silk, if she wasn't mistaken, and absolutely the most beautiful thing she'd ever owned, but just the thought of wearing it in this chilly flat gave her the shivers. Anyway, she didn't have anyone to wear it for.

She'd already opened the card that went with it, and read the bubbly letter it enclosed, full of the wedding plans so far. As she'd guessed, Sophia was spending the holiday with the family she would be joining in March.

As for her, with five years' difference in age between them they had spent too many years apart to be really close. It probably hadn't occurred to Sophia, floating around on her little pink cloud of happiness, that her little sister might be feeling a bit lonely in a new job in a new town.

'So what are you going to do about it?' she snapped suddenly, flipping the lingerie over the arm of the chair and tilting her chin up. 'Are you going to sit around feeling sorry for yourself or are you going to do something about it?'

She thought about the frozen meal waiting to be nuked into relative palatability and pulled a face.

'They're having turkey and all the trimmings up on Obs and Gyn, if it's anything like my last hospital,' she mused, considered her options for a moment longer and then reached for the phone.

'Well, all I can say is you're a glutton for punishment,' Jo said when Ella joined her little more than half an hour later. 'Not that I'm not glad to see you, but I think you are the only person I've ever known that's rung in on

Christmas Day to see if there's anything for them to do.'

'Actually, don't tell anyone, but it's all part of a clever plot so I don't have to cook myself a meal,' Ella said in a stage whisper. Jo would never guess just how much truth there was in the joke.

'Well, whatever the reason, I'm glad you rang when you did because I've got pregnant women coming out of my ears.'

'I've heard that this is the place for it,' Ella teased.

'Yes, but not all in labour at the same time,' Jo retorted. 'Honestly, the things some women will do to get out of spending Christmas with their families.'

Ella laughed, but to her own ears there was a slightly hollow sound to it. She would actually have loved to have had a big boisterous family surrounding her at this time of year. From what she could remember before Sophia had left home, there had been a lot of noise and colour and laughter. Ever since they'd lost their parents, the only 'family' she'd had to share the season with had been her hospital colleagues.

'Joking apart, what have you got that you want me to do?' Ella asked. 'Are any of the mums ones that I would remember from the hospital's antenatal classes?'

'One of them, I think. An older lady called Mrs Vincenti. Early forties, first baby, overweight, gestational diabetes.'

Ella groaned. 'How could I forget when you nicknamed her ''the walking disaster area''? The perfect example of everything that could go wrong and did.'

It wasn't quite true. At her age Maria Vincenti had been a prime candidate for the complication of a Down's syndrome baby, but the tests had given her the all-clear.

As for the rest of it, far too much was accurate.

Ever since she'd discovered that she was pregnant at long last, the volatile Italian restaurant owner had taken the old wives' tale of 'eating for two' to extremes. It hadn't been much of a surprise when her GP had notified them fairly early on in the pregnancy that he'd diagnosed gestational diabetes.

From that point on, her diet had been a battleground in which every skirmish won by the antenatal staff had been routed by a major counter-offensive. If human pregnancy hadn't been limited to nine months, Ella had wondered whether the woman might have eventually grown as wide as she was tall.

'She's full term?' Ella brought up the computer entry for her notes.

'Plus five days, much to her disgust,' Jo said with a chuckle then leant closer to confide. 'She actually came in on the due date demanding to know why she hadn't gone into labour. She said that she couldn't run a successful business if people didn't deliver when they said they would, and it was no wonder the health service was in such a state!'

Ella burst out laughing. That alone was enough to banish her blue mood.

'Did the midwife on duty point out that it was the patient's body at fault rather than our department?'

'Do you think it would have made any difference?' Jo countered, answering question with question.

'Having met Mrs V., not a bit.' Ella rolled her eyes. 'Ah, well, let's hope she doesn't find anything else to complain about while she's in labour.'

Just as she finished speaking there was a blood-curdling shriek that lasted for several mind-numbing seconds.

Ella cringed and whirled to face along the corridor towards the sound.

'What on earth was that?' she demanded with her heart pounding.

'*That* was Mrs Vincenti,' Jo said with a pained wince. 'Apparently she can remember her grandmother telling her that women shriek in labour to frighten the devil away. That way he won't be waiting around to pounce as soon as the head emerges.'

'Oh, my…' Ella sighed. 'I hope you've prepared some tactful explanations about what's going on for your patients.'

'Even better than that.' Jo held her hand out with a grin to reveal several packets of disposable earplugs. 'To conform to health and safety guidelines. They don't stop you hearing what she's saying, but they do stop your ears ringing when she starts shrieking.'

Ella tore open the little package and took out the little foam cylinders. It was the first time she'd ever had to resort to these measures, but she wasn't willing to take her chances spending any time next to a woman who sounded like Concorde taking off.

'Good morning, Mrs Vincenti,' she said brightly as she sailed into the room a moment later, cutting the latest shriek short by several blissful seconds.

'Where have you been?' Maria demanded instantly. 'I have been in this room for many hours with only a nurse. I am having a baby and I am in agony and nobody cares. You are the doctor who will make it come, yes?'

'I'm the midwife,' Ella corrected her, opting not to get into an argument about the length of time since she'd been admitted and the fact that the young woman she'd scathingly labelled as 'only a nurse' was a trainee midwife not far from the end of her course.

'You are not the *consulente*?' she exclaimed and burst into an over-excited flood of Italian, complete with windmilling arms.

Unfortunately, Ella couldn't speak Italian, but her mother had made sure that she understood enough to get by in an emergency.

'No, I'm not the *consulente*,' she confirmed, breaking into the recriminations firmly. 'I am a *levatrice*—' heaven only knew how she'd remembered the word but it had come to her just when she needed it '—who has delivered many babies and I will be looking after you until your little one arrives. Katy, here, is a fully qualified nurse who is nearly at the end of her training as a *levatrice*, and she will be extremely good at her job because she has small hands.'

Katy's eyebrows shot up towards her hairline at that recommendation and Ella had to look away or she would have giggled, but it was the effect on Maria Vincenti that was the most interesting.

'Small hands?' she repeated with a puzzled frown that suddenly cleared when she made the anatomical connection with what she was going through. 'Ah. Small hands,' she said again, her dark eyes going from one to the other as though comparing their comparative glove sizes.

There was no time for further conversation as the expression on the woman's face told them that another contraction was starting.

Before Ella could say anything she'd drawn in a deep breath and was shrieking at the top of her voice, pausing only to take in more air.

By the time the contraction died away Ella's ears were ringing in spite of the protection of the plugs. How Katy was coping after nearly half an hour of it, she didn't know. What she did know was that she was going to have to find some way to put a stop to it.

In spite of the antenatal clinic's best efforts, the woman was dreadfully overweight and was already panting and sweaty with at least an hour and probably more to go.

A glimmer of an idea slowly brightened, but how to present it?

'You come from the south of Italy?' she posed casually. 'From the country region?'

'Not at all,' she snapped as though mortally offended. 'I am from Bologna, in the north. More *sofisticato*. *Raffinato*. We have the oldest *università* in the world,' she said proudly, clearly affronted that Ella might have mistaken the fact.

'Well, that *is* strange,' Ella said with a frown and a slow shake of her head. 'I thought it was only in the south that the women hadn't learned about modern childbirth.'

She sent up a mental apology to all the wonderful modern medical establishments in the south of Italy and the thoroughly modern people who used them.

'What do you mean, *modern* childbirth? I am here and this is a modern hospital with all the modern methods, no?'

'Yes, but you are screaming in the old way. These days, we know that it will only waste your energy, making you too tired to help your baby to be born.'

'But I *must* scream. I must frighten away the *diavolo* so he will not get my baby.'

'Ah, but that is the old country way,' Ella said persuasively, speaking quickly because she knew that it wouldn't be much longer before another contraction started. 'These days, women stay as quiet as they can so they don't let the devil know that they are having a baby. They wait until the moment the head comes out and *then* they shout to scare him away.'

Ella watched the woman processing the information and marvelled that such a successful businesswoman should be so superstitious.

The expression on her face told them that she was definitely wavering so Ella brought out the final backup.

'The hospital also has a priest who can come to bless you and your baby when he arrives.'

'In the hospital?' she demanded suspiciously. 'He would come here?'

'Of course,' Ella confirmed. 'I could send a message for him now, if you like.'

Mrs Vincenti had a little time to think about her answer because a really strong contraction overtook her so powerfully that even without Ella's crafty mental gymnastics she didn't have the energy to scream.

'Breathe out,' Katy coached quietly. 'As if you're blowing out your baby's birthday candle. Don't fight the pain—it's doing an important job. Breathe in and blow out.'

Considering the woman had attended some of the antenatal classes, she seemed to have taken very little in, and Ella had to admire Katy's patience over the next hour.

The head was almost crowning when there was a minor disturbance outside in the department and a quick tap on the door.

'Mr Vincenti has arrived,' Jo told Ella, gesturing to the nervous-looking man behind her. 'He's not certain whether he's welcome to come in.'

Ella couldn't help smiling at him. He was so tall and painfully thin where his wife was absolutely the opposite.

'Of course he's welcome. Wait a moment while I get you a gown,' Ella said.

'No, no. You don't understand,' he said hurriedly, peering anxiously over Ella's shoulder into the room. 'I don't know whether my wife will want me to come in. It was not planned this way.'

'I can soon ask her. Just a moment.'

Ella hoped she'd managed to keep her curiosity out of her expression. While endlessly fascinating, the dynamics of other people's relationships were none of her business.

'Mrs Vincenti, would you like your husband to be here with you?' she asked, waiting till her patient was resting briefly between ferocious bursts of pushing. She had to give the woman her due. Once she'd had something explained to her she put her heart and soul into it.

'*Si.* I would love him to be here with me,' she said sadly. 'But it is not possible because we have the *ristorante*.'

Obviously her husband was listening for her reply, because it was followed by a rapid-fire burst of Italian that lit the exhausted woman's face up like a child in front of her first Christmas tree.

Ella understood just enough for tears to gather behind her eyes.

'What did he say?' Katy hissed when she'd helped the nervous man into a gown and sat him beside his tearfully smiling wife.

'He said that nothing, not even the restaurant, is more important than being with her when their baby is born. If I understood it right, he's dragged all their relatives in to take over the serving of sixty meals on Christmas Day just so he'd be free to come to the hospital.'

'Oh, wow!' Katy's eyes shone. 'Now we've *got* to make sure the baby arrives safely.'

Mr Vincenti had only just arrived in time for the event because within five minutes he was watching wide-eyed as his first child slithered uneventfully into the world with an indignant yell.

'*That* was enough to scare the *diavolo* away,' Maria Vincenti joked weakly, and Ella laughed.

'Seth said to tell you "well done",' Jo told her when the Vincentis had been transferred to the four-bedded bay closest to the nurses' station.

'Oh?' Ella couldn't help glancing around, not certain whether she was hoping to see him or hoping to avoid him.

'Apparently, they could hear Mrs V. vocalising all over the hospital and he came up to see if someone needed his help. Once he heard that you'd got the situation under control, he left. Mind you,' she added with a grin, 'he did say to give you full marks for ingenuity.'

'Knowing that gagging her would be seriously frowned upon, it was a choice of spinning her a believable yarn or losing my hearing,' Ella said wryly, hugging to herself the warm glow of pleasure at his approval.

That seemed to be the pattern of their working relationship over the next few weeks.

It didn't take long for Ella to realise that Seth seemed to be deliberately avoiding her.

He could hardly stay away from the department just because she was there, but where once he might have grabbed a cup of coffee and settled himself at one of the tables in the staff lounge to go over some paperwork or read a journal, now he left straight away.

No one else seemed to have noticed the difference but, then, they weren't the ones whose pulse rate doubled each time they heard his voice. They weren't the ones who went to bed each night reliving that mistletoe kiss.

Apart from spending less time on the unit, Ella slowly realised that Seth also seemed to be steering clear of being near her and even avoided talking to her unless strictly necessary, and that hurt.

Wasn't it bad enough that she was missing seeing him? Now she was also having to come to terms with the fact that she'd even lost the tentative friendship they'd started to form.

The trouble was, none of his efforts seemed to do anything to lessen the attraction she felt towards him. She was still convinced that she had found the man she had been waiting for all her life but, instead of being happy, she was miserable.

After more than two weeks of living on the frayed ends of her nerves she finally decided that she needed a break.

'Soph? It's Gabby,' she announced, having waited for her break to phone her sister's ward. 'What are you doing over the next couple of days?'

'Actually, I've been meaning to get in contact but everything's been so hectic that I haven't had a minute. When's your next long break between shifts? Could you come over and stay overnight so that we could put our heads together to choose your bridesmaid's dress?'

'Soph? Take a breath, please, and let me get a word in!' Ella teased. 'I'm finishing somewhere around three this afternoon and I'm not due back for two whole days.'

'Great!' Sophia exclaimed. 'Pack a bag. I'll pick you up and take you to the house. Be warned, though. All visitors are liable to get a paintbrush put in their hand.'

'House?' Ella repeated.

'Oh, Lord, is it really that long since we've spoken? I told you things have been chaos. David and I have bought a house…well, the bank owns most of it but they're letting us buy it off them a brick at a time for the next however many years.'

'So where is it and what is it like?' There was a sudden strange hollow inside her that echoed with loneliness and it was a real effort to sound genuinely interested.

Why did it seem as if everyone else was getting on with their lives and she was the only one standing still?

'You'll see it later this afternoon. With a bit of luck it will still be light enough to see the outside, but if not, we can do the grand tour of the stately acres—the size of a small pocket hankie—tomorrow. Oh,' she added as an afterthought, 'don't forget to bring some scruffy clothes. We could have a stripping party and some pizza tomorrow if we get the wedding outfits decided tonight.'

Ella put the phone down feeling almost as though she'd just been swung around a couple of times by a tornado then dropped on her head. And it would be even worse by the time she'd spent a couple of days in Sophia's company.

Still, she certainly wouldn't have time to mope if her sister was organising her activities, and she might even have the chance to ask for a little advice...purely hypothetically, of course. It wouldn't do to let Sophie know who she was attracted to or she might be tempted to give matters a sisterly nudge.

She stifled a groan, trying to imagine what Seth would think if Sophia tried to play match-maker; how he would react.

She'd probably have to move to a remote island somewhere in the middle of the Atlantic to live the embarrassment down. It had been bad enough when they had both been teen-agers, but now…It didn't bear thinking about.

'Sophie! It's gorgeous!' Ella exclaimed as soon as she saw the house. The light was fad-ing fast by the time they arrived, but it looked really pretty and compact and not at all mass-produced. 'However are you going to be able to afford something like this? I had no idea cardiac surgeons earned so much!'

'They don't, but between the two of us, we'll manage. Somehow!' She chuckled rue-fully while she hung coat and scarf over the end of the banisters and led the way into the lounge.

'It was called an ''affordable executive dwelling'' when it was built but the couple who bought it had problems,' she went on, and Ella was happy just to listen. It certainly helped to take her mind off things she'd rather forget.

'He had a major stroke and she wasn't physically strong enough to take care of him so they needed to move into some sort of place with nursing assistance on hand. They were looking for several months, getting more desperate all the time, then suddenly found a place near their son and wanted to get rid of this in a hurry.'

She whirled around happily in the middle of the as yet unfurnished but beautifully spacious room with her arms outstretched. 'We were lucky enough to be the first ones through the door with a reasonable amount of money to offer.'

'You certainly were lucky,' Ella agreed. 'You could fit my whole flat in this room. It's positively palatial.'

'And in answer to your other question,' Sophia continued pointedly, 'David and I will be buying it *together*. We've both got some savings and it'll be in our joint names, although what'll happen if we start a family…' She shrugged dismissively. 'That's a financial worry for another year. This year, with the house and the wedding, we're going to be absolutely flat broke.'

'But happy?' Ella prompted.

'But blissfully, ecstatically happy,' Sophia agreed. 'I've been in love with the wretched man ever since I met him and he'd barely done more than grunt at me over his mask. Then, out of the blue, he invited me out for a meal and went down on one knee.'

'What? Literally?' Ella's jaw dropped at the idea of staid, upright David doing anything so flamboyant.

'Yes, literally! In front of waiters, chefs and a restaurant full of diners! I nearly died of embarrassment on the spot!'

'But you said yes?'

'Of course I said yes! I was in love with the man. I *am* in love with him. Oh, Gabby, I'm just so happy. I only wish…'

She didn't finish but, then, she didn't need to. Ella could finish the thought for her because they both missed their parents, even though the years were going by and life had gone on. And then to have lost Granny Ruth as well, just a few months ago.

'If wishes were horses then beggars would ride,' Ella intoned in a bad imitation of that redoubtable lady's musical Scottish accent and Sophia burst out laughing, the sombre mood broken.

'Come on, there's the rest of the house to see, and then I'll show you the designs I've been looking at in the wedding books.'

She was off again, bubbling over with energy and high spirits, and as Ella followed in her wake *she* was the one left making hopeless wishes.

CHAPTER SEVEN

'SO WHAT do you think?' Sophie demanded an hour later, and Ella realised she hadn't a clue what her sister was talking about.

They'd taken the grand tour and giggled over the luxury of having a cloakroom, a bathroom *and* an *en suite*.

'Lucky girl. *Three* toilets to clean!' Ella had teased before sighing over the luxury of fitted cupboards with drawers that actually slid in and out easily.

Now they were back in the kitchen, picking over the crusts of what had once been a heavily laden pizza, but Ella's thoughts had wandered, in spite of her best efforts, to what it would be like if this were *their* house—hers and Seth's.

'What do I think?' she said, stalling for time, then had to make a stab in the dark. 'I think it's a beautiful house and by the time you've redecorated—'

'Not the house. The *dress*!' Sophie stabbed at a page in the magazine with a greasy finger. 'Come on. Keep up!' she teased.

'I like it, but not the bridesmaid's dress they suggest to go with it,' she said honestly, then paused, gratified that she already felt comfortable enough in her sister's company to speak her mind.

Perhaps they did still have a chance to form a closer, more adult friendship after all, she thought. Perhaps that would be better than trying to resuscitate the childhood relationship that had withered from disuse years ago.

Perhaps that was the way she was destined to go through her life, with lots of friends but none of them really close ones. It certainly seemed to be all that men wanted out of her, and one man in particular.

'I hate to admit it, but you're right about that dress,' Sophia confessed. 'It wouldn't do a thing for you. Far too fussy. So, how about that one instead?'

They were both relieved and delighted to find that they were on the same wavelength and it didn't take long before they'd settled on the styles they were looking for.

'Right, when are we going to hit the shops, then? Tomorrow morning?' Sophie suggested eagerly.

'With all the January sales on? Are you mad? I thought I'd been invited to do some decorating.'

'So what if the sales are on,' she exclaimed airily. 'Won't David be impressed with my thrift if I manage to get the price of my wedding dress reduced?'

'You're joking! Aren't you?' Ella still wasn't quite sure when her sister *was* joking and that was sad.

'Of course I am, but that doesn't mean that I wouldn't consider it if the dress I wanted was in the sale. It's not the price I pay for it that will make it perfect.'

The thought of fighting crowds of avid bargain-hunters when she could be chatting over a leisurely breakfast wasn't appealing. Even the hard physical labour of stripping dingy wallpaper would be preferable, but it was obviously what Sophia had set her heart on so Ella agreed with good grace.

'I'll also be calling in at the shop where I bought your Christmas present to look for something special for my honeymoon,' Sophia said with an attempt at insouciance that didn't quite come off when she blushed hotly.

'By all means let's look for something outrageously sexy for that first night,' Ella teased. 'Not that I think you're going to need it for a man daring enough to go down on his knees in public.'

'How about you?' Sophia demanded, neatly turning the tables. 'Have you worn your silky thing yet?'

'You must be joking! It's midwinter. I'd have frozen to death in my little flat.'

'Not if you had someone to keep you warm.'

'Central heating would be easier to arrange,' Ella retorted wryly. 'Finding someone to keep me warm would be all right if the one I wanted wanted me in return…'

'Oh, yes?' Sophia said, suddenly far too alert, and Ella realised she'd said much more than she'd intended. Her sister's antennae were up.

'Do you need some help? I've been there longer so I know whose ears to drop a few hints into.'

'No!' Ella gasped in horror. 'Don't even think about it.' She tried glaring at Sophia to get her point across but could see a scheming look in her sister's eyes.

'Soph, I mean it. Leave it alone,' she begged. 'He's already told me in words of one syllable that he's not interested.'

Her sister was quiet for a moment, obviously thinking things through.

'So he told you he wasn't interested. Was that before or after he slept with you?' she demanded out of the blue.

'Soph!' Suddenly, with her face blazing with heat, the idea of a closer relationship with this outrageous woman was becoming less attractive. 'We *didn't*...I haven't...' She couldn't even bring herself to say it.

'What? Never?' Sophia probed intently, taking liberties few people would have dared.

'I'm not saying anything more,' Ella declared uncomfortably. The fact that none of the men who'd wanted to sleep with her had interested her was not something that she was going to apologise for. 'Now, didn't you say something about decorating? Is there some preparation we could do this evening to get started?'

'Spoilsport,' her sister taunted then allowed the topic to be changed with a teasing pretence of reluctance. 'Actually I was hoping to get a few tips for March.'

It was her turn to go scarlet and all Ella could do was gape. She'd thought she was enough of an oddity not to have slept with a man at her age, but her sister was five years older.

'What—you, too?' she exclaimed with a weak attempt at laughter. 'I bet Mama's up in heaven with her halo shining. She certainly managed to stress the benefits of virginity in a way that stuck.'

'The trouble is, we're now left to cope with the disadvantages of it,' her sister said gloomily. 'Not only do we have to work out *how* to tell the man of our dreams that they're going to be the first, but we've also got to decide *when* to tell him.'

At least you know yours will be listening, Ella thought later that night, snuggled down in the toasty warmth of what would eventually be the guest room. Mine doesn't even want to know that he's the man of my dreams.

There was a new closeness between the two of them after that mad, hectic weekend that changed something elemental inside Ella.

She wasn't absolutely certain what it was. There had always been the family connection between herself and Sophia, but for the first time since her sister had left home to start her nursing training, she didn't feel quite so…so *alone*.

Whatever it was, she was conscious of a new confidence in herself that seemed to spill over into her time at work.

Somehow, little by little over the next month, she and Seth seemed to regain most of the ground they'd lost with that kiss.

It began in small ways with an answered greeting or the offer of a cup of coffee, but eventually they'd graduated to sitting together and swapping tales of the trials of being a younger sibling.

Even so, there was something that niggled at the back of Ella's mind.

She didn't know if it was because she really cared about Seth that made her sensitive to the nuances of his behaviour, but she became increasingly aware that there was something, some secret that was gnawing away at him from the inside.

Several times she'd come upon him in the staff lounge staring out of the window looking as if he had the weight of the world on his shoulders. Her heart ached for him and she couldn't help offering tea and sympathy but he never so much as mentioned whatever was preying on his mind.

All she could do was find something lighthearted to talk about to bring him out of the depression in the hope that either the problem would eventually resolve itself or that he would trust her enough to confide in her.

One topic that was almost guaranteed to lighten his mood was the progress towards Sophia's big day.

She'd told him everything about the shared traumas from the very first outing to try on dresses at the height of the January sales.

In fact, her description of that day was the very first time that she'd ever heard him laugh out loud, the husky sound almost rusty as though it hadn't been used much recently.

Still, the mental images she'd been painting of vicious, crazed women ripping dresses out of each other's hands regardless of size or suitability, just because they had the largest price reduction, was a memory she wasn't going to forget in a hurry.

And the countdown to the event was relentless, calculable in hours now, rather than days and weeks.

Bearing in mind the fact that Sophia and David had a fairly large circle of friends within the hospital community, they'd initially racked their brains for a way to invite the maximum number without bankrupting themselves.

In the end, they'd settled for an intimate ceremony in the hospital chapel limited strictly to family members, followed by a similarly small reception in a local hotel. In the evening there was going to be a less formal party to which the rest of their colleagues were invited.

'How small is small?' Seth enquired lazily, yawning as he stretched after a particularly time-consuming repair job in Theatre. 'For some people with large extended families that could be anything up to fifty.'

'That sounds like a nightmare when you're organising something like this,' Ella exclaimed. 'I can't imagine how anyone would cope.'

'*They* probably wouldn't be able to cope with the idea of inviting half the staff of a hospital,' he pointed out logically. 'So, how many will this be?'

Ella had been waiting for a chance to lead up to this for several days now, ever since she'd been handed an ultimatum by her sister.

'Either you ask someone, or I'll find you an escort myself,' she'd declared last night, her voice no less forceful for coming at Ella down a phone line.

'Well, on their side, there'll be David and his parents, his brother, who's best man, and his wife. On ours, there's Sophia with me as her bridesmaid.'

'That sounds as if your side is rather outgunned. Aren't there any other relatives you can dig out of the woodwork?'

'Not one, in spite of the fact that Mum was Italian. She had a sister who became a nun in an enclosed order, and a brother who was a parish priest in Turin. Dad didn't have any brothers or sisters.'

She paused for a moment to gather her courage and remember the words she'd practised, knowing she wasn't going to get a better chance than this.

'Actually, Seth, Sophia's been nagging me to ask…if you'd be my escort for the day.'

There. The words were out. Now all she had to do was cross her fingers that he'd accept.

'Your escort?' he said, peering at her through one half-opened eye. 'What would that involve?'

'Well, mostly it's a case of evening up the numbers, because the rest of them will all be in couples. But it does mean that you get a free meal at an expensive hotel and an evening of dancing.'

'What would I have to wear?' he demanded warily, both eyes open now. 'Not a blasted penguin suit, I hope.'

That meant Seth was actually considering it!

Her heart danced a silly little jig inside her in spite of all her stern admonitions.

'Absolutely no penguin suits allowed! Ordinary two- or three-piece with collar and tie.'

'And no senile great-great-aunts with whom to hold shouted conversations?'

'Not one,' she promised with a grin as pleasure blossomed within.

'And I take it you've already checked to see if I'm on call that day, and were perfectly prepared to beg me to do what ever it took to rearrange it,' he said wryly.

'Of course,' she agreed, knowing that her eyes must be shining.

'And Sister Buchan would extract a terrible vengeance if you didn't persuade me?'

'Indubitably.' Ella did like this playful side of his character. It didn't emerge nearly often enough.

'In that case, I'd better agree forthwith. It looks as if you've got yourself an escort for the wedding.'

'Are you sorry you came yet?' Ella demanded out of the side of her mouth as they posed for yet another photo.

'Not yet,' he confirmed. 'I'm still enjoying seeing what everyone looks like when they're not wearing surgical scrubs.'

The approval in Seth's eyes when he'd first seen the outfit she and Sophia had chosen had left her basking in a warm glow. She knew the coppery bronze fabric picked up similar glints in her hair but it was the flattering cut of the fluid fabric that made her feel good wearing it.

There was laughter in his voice as they talked. It didn't sound nearly so rusty these days but it still didn't happen nearly often enough for her liking.

The trouble was, that deep husky sound was just another facet of the man that set her hormones in an uproar, whatever she tried to do to subdue them.

Take his appearance, for example. How was she supposed to keep her emotions on an even keel when Seth turned up wearing a classic charcoal grey suit with a silk shirt and tie just one shade paler, and then opened the jacket to reveal a tartan waistcoat?

The fact that the tartan exactly matched the long sash she had draped over one shoulder in honour of their Buchanan forebears couldn't be a coincidence. The fact that he must have deliberately searched it out touched her deeply.

'I love the waistcoat,' she murmured when she had the threat of tears under control.

'Well, it was either this one, the one covered in naked ladies or the hand-embroidered one featuring a forest scene full of jungle animals.'

She gave a gurgle of laughter, instantly diverted. 'I don't believe it! Naked ladies?'

'No, I thought it was too much of a good thing, too. After all, I'm seeing them all day,' he said with wicked nonchalance. 'Actually, that's why my brother gave it to me...when I told him what specialty I was thinking of.'

'You mean it actually exists!'

'Do you doubt it? Perhaps you want me to wear it to work one day.'

'Don't you dare! You'd probably be sacked. It wouldn't be so bad if it were on your underwear, but a waistcoat...' She shook her head, still not certain that she believed him.

'Now you've got designs on my underwear?' he demanded in a scandalised voice, and she was laughing again, marvelling at this new side of his character. In all the weeks that she'd known him she'd never heard him talk in such a flirtatious way. Was it because this was a social event totally separate from their daily work?

Whatever the reason for his light-hearted mood, she was delighted. It was just what she'd needed to stop her dwelling on all the people who couldn't be here today.

'Don't look now, but I think the photographer's finally finished,' Seth muttered as the man in question began fitting his precious camera into an expensive-looking case and the small group began to scatter. 'Is this the point where we can relax and get in our cars?'

'Only until we get to the hotel. What's the betting he'll be lying in wait to get a shot of them cutting the cake?'

'As long as he doesn't mind catching me in the background shovelling food in. I'm starving,' he complained. His stomach chose that precise moment to rumble loudly and Ella was laughing again.

As Ella got ready for the dance that evening her emotions were in turmoil.

She'd spent most of the day in Seth's company, much of it laughing, but it had been those other times that had left her on edge.

The first time had been when she'd been following Sophia into the little hospital chapel and had realised that, instead of watching the bride, Seth's eyes had been following her. She'd been too far away to read his expression then, but later, during their meal, she'd noticed several times that there had been another emotion hidden behind the smiles.

Towards the end of the reception he'd stopped to have a word with the newly-weds and it had only been when she'd heard her sister insisting that his presence was essential at the dance that evening that she'd realised that he'd actually been trying to make his excuses.

Now here she was dressed in all her finery with her make-up as perfect as she could make it, and she was scared to join the rest of the wedding party. In fact, she was terrified to find out how much it was going to hurt if Seth wasn't there.

'Are you ready, Gabby?' Sophia called as she tapped on the door.

Ella threw one last look around the room, contemplating the likelihood that she could manufacture a sudden migraine so that she could hide out in these luxurious surroundings.

'Coward!' she muttered, straightening her shoulders and lifting her chin. 'Don't you dare *think* about doing anything to spoil Sophia's day. Anyway, if you're lucky, you'll actually be able to claim that dance from Seth.'

She drew in a deep breath and reached for the little credit-card sized piece of plastic that would let her back in at the end of the day.

'Am I ready?' she said as she flung the door open. 'What do you think?'

The first of the guests had already started arriving when the wedding party stepped out of the lift, but the only person Ella saw was Seth.

'Sorry I didn't get back in time to escort you from your room,' he murmured as he offered his arm. 'I had a visit to make and was delayed.'

Ella was so relieved that he was there that it was several moments before she realised how tense he was. The muscles in his arm felt like iron, almost as though he was having to steel himself against her touch.

'Seth?' she whispered uncertainly, loosening her hold on him.

'Shh,' he whispered back, similarly conscious that they were now being ushered into a reception line and their words might be overheard.

He caught her hand in his and replaced it on his arm with a gentle squeeze. 'I'm sorry. Problems on my mind. I should learn to switch off.'

He smiled down at her but, although he was trying hard to hide it, she was becoming too adept at reading him to miss his preoccupation.

There was no chance for any further private conversation as they were submerged under a series of waves of colleagues, each eager to greet the newly-weds. By the time they reached Ella and Seth on the end they were ready to talk shop and it didn't take very long before the formality of a reception line degenerated into a happy welcoming mêlée.

Finally, David's father grabbed a glass and tapped it with a knife.

'I'm not going to make a speech,' he announced to cheerful laughter, 'but now that we've welcomed Sophia into our family I feel like I can take over some of the duties that her father would have performed. In this case, it's to invite you all to gravitate towards the buffet whenever you're ready. After that, we'll get the two of them to cut the cake and the dancing can begin. In the meantime, we'd like to thank all of you for coming to share this happy day with us.'

The round of applause that followed set the tone for the evening. Everyone Ella spoke to seemed genuinely happy for her sister and were thoroughly enjoying the party.

As predicted, the photographer reappeared just in time to make a full-scale production out of cutting the cake, but Ella barely noticed. She was filled with rapidly growing anticipation as the time for her long-awaited dance with Seth drew nearer.

Her first chance of getting Seth to redeem his promise had been ruined by the announcement of Sophia's impending wedding. That made it seem somehow fitting that it should finally be fulfilled at that wedding.

Not that she hadn't tried to claim it in the interim. She'd actually attended the Valentine's Day dance at the end of a twelve-hour shift in the hope that she might be able to dance with him.

She hadn't even been sure that he would be there, knowing that he'd disappeared from the unit around six o'clock, muttering something about being late.

As if he'd been waiting for her to arrive, he'd been standing near the door surrounded by a plethora of pink and red hearts and, true to their reinstated friendship, she'd felt perfectly free to walk up to him to claim the next dance.

They'd even got as far as walking onto the floor before his pager had called him away and Ella had begun to wonder if they were fated never to dance together. She'd seen how well he'd moved with other women and couldn't wait to know the all-too-rare pleasure of partnering a man who really knew how to dance.

The band struck up, beginning with a waltz especially for David and Sophia.

Ella's eyes prickled as she watched them slowly whirling around the floor together. There was an almost dream-like perfection to the scene with the tall blond man in his dark suit cradling the elegant auburn-haired woman in the slender flowing ivory dress.

'Ready to join them?' Seth murmured in her ear and Ella's heart turned a somersault.

It dropped straight into her strappy sandals when she heard a pager go off and realised that it was Seth's.

'Not again!' she wailed as he made his apologies and hurried away.

It was several minutes before he returned, minutes in which Ella had begun to wonder if she was ever going to dance with the man.

'He isn't on call, so why was his pager going off?' she muttered crossly. 'And why did he even have his pager with him in the first place?'

Her heart leapt anew when she saw him making his way into the room again. She hurried to meet him, eager to claim him at last, but then she saw the expression on his face.

'Seth?' she murmured, drawing him unobtrusively to one side. 'What's the matter?'

He looked shattered…or battered?

Whatever had happened in the few minutes since he'd left the room, it had obviously hit him hard and her heart went out to him.

'I'm sorry. It's…' He shook his head, clearly unwilling or unable to go on.

'Bad news?' She couldn't think of any patients that would cause this effect. He tended to become more involved than most consultants, probably because he was dealing with something as special as childbirth, but she'd never seen him like this before.

'Yes,' he said then paused to sigh heavily. 'No. Not really, but still…'

'Is there something you need to do? Somewhere you need to go? Would you like to leave? I could always make your apologies to—'

'Yes… No… Oh, God, I don't know,' he said indecisively, obviously rattled. He shook his head then groaned and ran his fingers through his hair in a gesture of exasperation.

Just then the bandleader announced a Latin selection and Ella's ears pricked up in spite of the fraught situation with Seth.

His mouth twisted wryly. 'I promised you a dance months ago, didn't I? How good are you at Latin-American?'

'Tango?' The familiar beat was already making her feet itch.

'Competition or Argentinian?' he said, and it sounded almost like throwing down a gauntlet.

'Oh, Argentinian, every time,' she replied, surprising herself with a husky laugh. 'If you think you're up to it.'

His bow took her by surprise, as did the way he took her hand to lead her out onto the floor. He was a tall dark-haired Englishman, but just for a moment he'd looked every inch the flamboyant Latin, right up to the proud way he held his head.

The tango had been one of the last dances Ella had learned when she'd still had time to go to classes, and it was the one that never failed to stir her senses.

The Argentinian form had developed in a region where the men greatly outnumbered the women, so that the most popular man on the dance floor would be the one who made his partner shine.

For this to happen, the two would have to find some deep elemental connection when they began to move to the music that would allow each to know instinctively what the other wanted.

Ella had heard about this elemental connection but until Seth took her into his arms she had doubted that it really existed.

It was almost like finding the other half to herself, the part that had been missing the whole of her life and without which she would never be complete.

The music swirled around them, the tempo echoing the beat of their hearts as they stepped, swayed and turned in perfect harmony. Every inch of her body was aware of him, their bodies meeting, brushing, taunting in a ritual that evoked more primitive activities.

For several electric beats of the music he held her poised in his arms, her weight pivoted on the ball of one foot while her body draped seductively across his.

Ella gazed up into the mysterious grey of his eyes and when she recognised the searing heat they held she breathed in sharply.

Her senses were teased by the faint scent of the soap he'd used earlier in the day and something more individual, something that belonged just to Seth.

The dance continued but their connection was so strong by now that she could follow his every move without thought, their bodies so attuned that they could have been dancing together for years.

This is it, she thought exultantly as they gazed into each other's eyes, oblivious of anyone or anything else in the room beyond the music. This must be that once-in-a-lifetime partnership her dance teacher had told her about. The bond that went far beyond mere physical compatibility to unite heart and soul as well.

Then Seth brought their bodies together again, joining them from shoulder to thigh to execute a series of fast and intricate steps. They didn't miss a beat, even when she realised that, like his, her body was reacting to their proximity and the passion of the dance.

It was all in his eyes, as she was sure it must be in hers—the initial surprise and confusion, followed by pleasure and enjoyment that escalated into exultation.

By the time the music reached the final throbbing chord she was breathless and her body was electric with adrenaline but all she could think of was the fact that, at this moment, he wanted her every bit as much as she wanted him.

'Fantastic!' someone shouted and they jerked out of the spell that had wound around them to find themselves alone in the middle of the floor surrounded by applauding colleagues.

Seth rolled his eyes at her but she could tell by the rising colour along his cheekbones that he wasn't quite as nonchalant about being the centre of attention as he appeared.

'Do we duck and run, or what?' he murmured.

'How about a bow for the judges?' she suggested, and suited her actions to her words before they tried to make their way towards her sister.

It was a bit like running the gauntlet with all the exclamations and compliments that were showered on them, but it all faded away when she concentrated on the protective arm Seth had wrapped around her shoulders.

There was teasing about the possibility of changing careers when they reached their table but Ella was almost oblivious to it, far more conscious of the tension that had built up between them on the floor and was still humming between them.

She chanced a glance at him and found Seth watching her, his eyes darker and more intent than ever, and her heart missed a beat.

For several timeless seconds he gazed silently at her as though trying to come to a decision, then he leaned closer.

'I need to speak to you,' he said hoarsely, catching hold of her hand and clasping it tightly with his, then glancing over her shoulder at the throng surrounding them in the room. 'Can we leave for a while or do you still have duties to perform?'

It took Ella a moment to get her thoughts in order.

'No more duties.' She shook her head with an uncertain smile. 'Soph needed me to get her into her dress, but it's up to David to get her out of it. I'll just have a quick word with her. OK?'

'OK, but—'

'I won't be long,' she promised and stood up on shaky legs that had nothing to do with their recent dance.

He seemed very intent and an unexpected shiver slid up her spine to raise the hairs on the back of her neck. She had a sudden feeling that he was going to tell her something she didn't want to know, something that would change the relationship between them for ever.

'Soph?' She'd had to wait a minute to speak to her and was overwhelmingly aware of each passing second.

'Hey, Gabby!' Sophia exclaimed with a happy smile, beckoning her closer. 'Nice to see that those years of dancing lessons paid off in the end. I've never seen you do it better.'

'Thanks, Soph, but… Would you mind if I were to cut out on you? Seth was bleeped a little while ago. I think it was bad news. Anyway, he wants to talk and…'

'After that dance I'd be very surprised if all he wanted to do was talk!' she teased, much to Ella's embarrassment. Thank goodness there was no one close enough to overhear.

'Soph! We aren't… You know we don't have that sort of relationship.'

'Well, I definitely think you ought to be thinking about it. If he's that good a mover on the floor, just imagine what he'll be like between the sheets!'

Ella was still spluttering when Sophia waved her off.

'If I see you again this evening, well and good. If not, we'll see you when we get back from honeymoon.'

Ella made her way across the floor with one part of her mind concerned about what Seth was going to talk about. Unfortunately, the other part was still replaying her sister's teasing words in glorious Technicolor.

CHAPTER EIGHT

SETH was waiting anxiously for Ella to appear, his impatience made worse by apprehension.

'This is stupid,' he muttered as he tugged at his collar then thrust his hands into his pockets.

Why on earth had he suggested talking to her? He knew it was too soon to be holding this conversation, and he'd been mad to have suggested it tonight, but after all these months he'd suddenly been struck by a desperate need to talk.

That could only have resulted from that final phone call, the call that had told him that the situation he'd been living with had finally, painfully resolved itself.

For the first time in a long time—much longer than he cared to think about—there was actually light at the end of the tunnel, and he hoped that Ella was the one holding it.

For the moment, though, there were still an awful lot of problems to be resolved. Too many. Perhaps he should just leave a message for her to say that he'd had to leave…

Too late.

There she was coming out of the room now, the fluid fabric of her dress and the coppery bronze colour making her look like a column of living flame and setting every hormone in his body on fire.

She caught sight of him and the way her face lit up was unbelievable. How could he have been so lucky to have met someone like her?

If only it hadn't happened at this time in his life. It had been hell seeing her and working with her on a daily basis, knowing that nothing could come of it. Knowing that he had to hide his attraction, pretend it didn't exist.

Tonight, holding her in his arms and moving with her to the rhythm of the music, that had been impossible.

But how could he have known that she could dance like that? Perhaps he should have guessed after that solitary disastrous kiss under the mistletoe that it would be like putting a match to tinder, but he'd thought they would be safe in front of all those people.

What people? Once he'd had her in his arms the rest of the world had ceased to matter…ceased to exist. The only thing that had been relevant had been that Ella had been as close to him as two layers of clothing would allow, moving with him as if she were the other half of his soul.

'Sorry to keep you waiting,' she murmured as she drew near, with that endearing touch of shyness that always made his gut clench with desire. She seemed so innocent, so untouched, and yet the expression in those green eyes of hers when she'd gazed up into his on the dance floor had been as old as Eve.

How was he ever going to be able to find the words to tell her about his tangled life—about the disappointments and tension and about the ultimate tragedy?

The only thing he was certain about, as he stood to greet her and breathed in the scent of wildflowers that always surrounded her, was that he would have to tell her all about it if there was to be any chance of the relationship he wanted. His own sense of honesty wouldn't allow him to do anything less.

'Where do you want to talk?'

Ella's heart was in her throat, almost blocking the innocuous words. His eyes were so dark and his gaze so intense that they almost stopped her from being able to speak at all.

'I don't know.' Seth gazed around the hotel's reception area and realised that, although there were several chairs grouped about for the convenience of their patrons, the whole room was far too public for his needs. It was going to be hard enough telling her about the mess his life had become without worrying about eavesdroppers.

'I don't know,' he admitted, shifting uneasily from one foot to the other. 'It's still much too cold to go for a walk, even with a coat on over your dress.'

The way his eyes slid over her was as potent as a caress and her pulse rate climbed another notch.

'We could talk upstairs,' she offered tentatively, avoiding his eyes lest he was able to divine the way her sister's words had suddenly leapt into her head. There was a bed in her room upstairs—two, in fact, and either of them ideal for finding out if Seth's dancing was as good as his…

'Upstairs?' he repeated, his voice grown deeper, huskier and more than enough to fuel the fantasy. 'You're staying here?'

'Just for two nights,' she explained hastily, the luxurious establishment far outside her budget. 'David's family are staying here and insisted on booking a suite for Sophia and I to share last night. She won't be needing it tonight.' The final words ended in a whisper when she realised how they might sound.

A heavy silence stretched in the wake of her words, fraught with unspoken dangers and possibilities, before he wordlessly gestured towards the bank of lifts.

She was quivering deep inside by the time the doors slid shut and so impossibly tense that when he cleared his throat she nearly jumped out of her skin.

'Ella?'

The sound of her name in his voice was like having velvet stroked over her skin, soothing and arousing at the same time.

'Ella, you have to press the button,' he prompted gently, and she nearly groaned aloud with embarrassment.

The lift couldn't read her mind but she had an uncomfortable feeling that Seth could. It must be written in big bold letters that her invitation up to her room was directing her thoughts along just one path.

The soft ping warned that the doors were going to open and she stepped out into the corridor.

'This way,' she said as she turned, the key-card ready in her hand.

'Ella, are you sure about this?' he asked, putting his hand over hers when she would have inserted the card in the slot.

The contact was electric and she couldn't hold back a soft gasp.

Since they'd left the dance floor, it was almost as though they'd been avoiding touching each other.

Until now.

She looked up into his face and saw the confirmation she needed. He was just as affected by this strange emotional connection as she was, just as aroused by the physical contact, no matter how small and insignificant.

Ella didn't know what he'd seen in her eyes but when his hand tightened over hers she was flooded with the realisation that this could be the moment she'd been waiting for.

On the surface, they'd come up here because Seth had said that he needed to talk to her, but it seemed as if he needed *her* even more.

'Come in, Seth,' she whispered unsteadily and released the lock, finally certain that she was doing the right thing. 'Please, come in.'

It was several seconds before he took the steps that brought him into the softly lit room and she hadn't realised just how unsure she'd been that he would until she heard the click as the door closed behind him.

'Do you want to sit down?' she invited. In spite of her new certainty, the words still shook with nervous tension in the sudden silence that stretched between them. 'There's tea or coffee, or I could get you something from the mini-bar.'

'Ella.'

The sound of her name was enough to stop her chattering, especially when it sounded as if it had been dragged out of him that way.

'Yes?' She drew in a quivering breath and finally turned to face him fully.

'I don't want a drink, I just need…' Words failed him but she could read what he wanted in his eyes, knew what he wanted because it was what she wanted too.

This was the man she'd been falling in love with since the first time she'd seen him, and the emotion had only been growing deeper and stronger with each passing day.

And here and now, for whatever reason, the defences he'd tried to erect against her had fallen so that she could see clearly that he felt the same way.

'Oh, Seth,' she whispered, suddenly finding the courage to take that first step towards him, the first step that would take her into his arms. 'Oh, Seth, hold me, please. Kiss me.'

There was the briefest second of hesitation, as though she'd taken him by surprise, but then he was there, cupping one hand around her cheek while he gazed at her as if he couldn't believe what was happening.

'Ah, Ella, I know I promised you a dance, but—'

'Then dance with me again, Seth,' she begged, suddenly afraid that he was going to stop the conflagration she wanted before it started. 'Dance with me now, the way you did downstairs.'

She held her hand out to him and with a groan he took it and pulled her slowly towards him, stopping when there were just a precious few inches between them.

'Are you sure, Ella?' he demanded softly, his eyes caressing her face. 'You have to be certain because it might start off as a dance, but it won't end there.'

Her heart thumped unevenly and she drew in a ragged breath.

'Oh, yes, Seth. I'm sure,' she said fervently and closed the distance between them, her arms lifting to circle his neck, her fingers tangling in the thick silky strands of his hair the way they'd been longing to do.

'Then give me your mouth,' he groaned as his head came down towards her. 'Oh, God, I need your sweetness.'

He brushed his lips over hers, gently, almost tentatively, over and over again, then pressed more firmly, but it wasn't enough for either of them. This time, without an audience looking on, their bodies were even closer than they had been on the dance floor, their mouths beginning a tentative exploration that could have but one result.

'Open for me, Ella,' he growled, nipping gently then soothing the place with his tongue. 'Let me in.'

She complied willingly, knowing from their mistletoe kiss up on the ward that it was an invitation to the entry of his tongue, knowing that it was going to lead to so much more.

Her tongue met his, hesitantly at first then more boldly, thrusting and parrying in the velvet dark intimacy until her knees grew weak.

As if he knew her strength was gone his arms wrapped convulsively around her, drawing her up against his body so that she was almost lifted off her feet.

She could feel his heart beating against her breasts, every bit as fast as her own, and felt too the extent of his arousal. Instinctively she pressed her hips against him, testing his response, and when he groaned aloud she froze for a second before doing it again.

'Ah, stop, sweetheart. Help me,' he muttered against her mouth, and suddenly they were both fighting with buttons and zips, all hesitation gone as the urgency grew beyond control.

It would only have taken him moments to peel her out of her elegant dress and less than that to discard the silky panties but with Ella trying to fumble with a row of tiny buttons to open his shirt it was taking far too long.

'Leave that for next time,' he growled as he lifted her so that she could wrap her legs around his hips, and then she heard the unmistakable rasp of his zip.

'Can't wait,' he groaned almost incoherently as he pressed her naked back against the cold wall, his whole body shaking with the violence of his need. 'Ella…Forgive me…I can't wait…' And he cried out in a mixture of agony and ecstasy as he joined their bodies together for the first time.

Ella thought she'd known what to expect but this was so much more than any book she'd read. This wasn't the romance of soft music and candlelight, this was all the passion and fury of a storm at sea and she was helpless to resist.

It didn't matter that she had no idea how to respond, her body knew, coaching her into moving with Seth and against him as the tempest escalated into a hurricane and then the lightning finally struck and demolished the world.

Neither of them had breath to speak, and his body was still bracing hers against the wall when he pressed his forehead to hers.

'If it gets any better than this, woman, I won't survive,' he rumbled gruffly in her ear then dipped his head to brush a tender kiss across her lips.

Ella couldn't help her body's reaction to the caress and the heat swept up her throat and into her face when he instantly groaned in reaction, deepening the kiss and the contact between their bodies.

She hadn't realised that he had moved out of the lounge area of the suite into the bedroom until, long seconds later, he lowered the two of them onto one of the enormous beds without ever breaking the contact between them.

Ella felt herself drifting into consciousness with a smile on her face, still savouring the most explicit dream she'd ever had about Seth Gifford, when she heard a noise in the other half of the suite.

Her brain was still scrambling to make sense of the sound and her unexpected surroundings when her memory finally woke up.

Her eyes flew open and she scrabbled reflexively for a sheet to pull over her totally naked body.

'It wasn't a dream,' she whispered aloud as she gazed swiftly around the room, somehow needing to hear the words to make them true. The jumble of bedclothes scattered on the floor and the lacy bra dangling from the arm of the nearby chair should have been enough to kick-start her memory.

'Oh, my…!' She pulled the sheet over her face to hide her blushes when she recalled the way she'd made the first advances, inviting him into her room, asking him to kiss her…and the way he'd reciprocated…pinning her against the wall!

And that had been just the beginning.

It had been hours before they'd finally fallen asleep in each other's arms, only to wake again as the first grey light of dawn had begun to brighten the room.

That had been hours ago, but she could still remember her gasp at the first contact of naked skin on naked skin.

She'd been stunned by the searing heat that had poured out of him. He was so…so big. Long-limbed, broad-shouldered and powerful, one minute taking her as though they were two elemental animals caught up in a ferocious mating ritual, but the next so gentle, so caring, touching her as if she were the most precious thing in the world.

But where was he, this multifaceted man who had initiated her into the world of desire? She was sure she'd heard him in the other room of the suite as she'd woken up.

'Seth?' she called as she dragged her fingers through the tangled strands of her hair to try to subdue it into some sort of order. Heaven only knew where her make-up had gone. Probably, half of it was on the bedclothes and the other half on the towels after their dead-of-night shower together.

'Seth,' she called again, and when there was still no answer she wrapped the sheet around herself and went looking.

'He's gone,' she said in utter disbelief, having searched the tiny suite in a matter of seconds. And there was no sign of a note either.

She was about to look down the back of the bed in case he'd placed a note on the pillow when the illuminated numbers on the bedside clock caught her eye.

She sagged onto the bed with relief.

'Of course he's not here, you ninny! He's gone to work.'

She would have preferred him to have woken her up before he'd left, just so that she could have given him a kiss goodbye…but on second thoughts, if he'd done that, he'd probably still be here!

'Incredible!' she whispered with a giggle. 'Yesterday a virgin, today insatiable!' And she was already looking forward to the next time as she padded into the bathroom.

She emerged just in time to wave Sophia and David off on their honeymoon, and was grateful that her sister was too wrapped up in her own happiness to notice the matching whisker burn Ella had collected during the night.

The rest of the day was definitely an anti-climax, especially when she didn't hear from Seth, but that was nothing compared to the next morning.

'Seth… Mr Gifford's gone?' she repeated numbly when Carol gave them the news at the start of their shift. 'Gone where?'

'No idea, nor if he'll be coming back. Just that he's applied to take all his accumulated leave at short notice. What a good job you managed to have your dance with him.'

'Dance?' It seemed to have happened light years ago.

'Yes, you dark horse. I never knew you could dance like that. How long have you been having lessons?'

Ella knew she must have given some sort of answer but all she was conscious of was feeling sick.

'Well, if we keep standing around chatting we'll be given the sack. At least with your dancing you've got another skill. The rest of us need the jobs we've got.'

Ella knew that she did her job well that day because professional pride wouldn't let her do anything else, but it was when she was on her breaks that the hurt seeped past her defences and threatened her equanimity.

Over the next few weeks Seth's name came up frequently as his patients were allocated to other members of the team, but she hadn't realised that she was reacting to it in any special way until one of the midwives, newly returned from an extended maternity leave, called her aside for a moment.

'Ella, I know all about patient confidentiality, but she's not really a patient, and I hope you don't think I'm being nosy for the sake of it but…' Lena paused uncomfortably after her rambling introduction.

'Go on,' Ella invited, suddenly struck by a sinking premonition of disaster. 'If you want to know something I can't tell you, then I won't.'

'Well, it's just… I knew Seth when we both worked at my last hospital. All three of us, actually. His wife is in Obs and Gyn, too.'

'His wife?' Ella echoed weakly as her whole fantasy world shattered silently around them.

Seth was *married*?

She'd spent the most magical night of her life committing adultery?

'Yes. She was absolutely desperate to have a baby and two cycles of IVF treatment had already failed. I knew she had frozen embryos left from the first collection and she made no bones about being eager to have another try so… Did she finally manage to have her baby or is there another problem? Is that why Seth's had to go on leave?'

'Lena, I have absolutely no idea,' she said honestly, self-discipline the only thing that stopped her from howling out her hurt. 'All we were told was that he was taking some leave but not why. There was certainly no mention of a baby or even his wife.'

'Damn,' Lena muttered. 'That's one of the things I hated about going on maternity leave. It's a bit like taking a book back to the library without reading the last chapter. There are all those women I'd got to know, and I never saw them have their babies.'

Ella made sympathetic noises but her heart wasn't in it. How could it be when it had just been wrenched out of her chest and torn asunder?

The rest of the day was difficult, especially as they were quiet and there was too much time to think.

Not that endless hours of thinking solved anything. She still had no idea whether Seth was ever coming back or what she would say to him if he did.

In the end, the decision was almost taken for her, with the news that her grandmother's will had finally passed through probate.

'Come and stay for the weekend, Gabby,' Sophia invited, the joy in her voice coming down the telephone in waves. 'We promise to behave ourselves with the utmost propriety in your company, but we really need to talk about what we want to do about the croft.'

It was more than three weeks since the wedding and both of them were back at work, but Ella suddenly felt the need to spend some time with her sister away from the hothouse atmosphere of the hospital. Perhaps her appetite would return.

'I'd love to come,' she said fervently. 'Do I need to bring my working clothes with me or have you finished the decorating?'

'Bring them, please! If it's wet we can decorate but if it's dry we can start on the garden.'

'Slave driver,' Ella teased, the heaviness around her heart already a little lighter at the prospect of a change of scenery.

* * *

The weight returned with a vengeance on Friday morning when she'd barely put her feet to the floor before she had to rush to the toilet.

It was a depressingly simple job to buy a pregnancy detector kit from the chemist on the way to work, and it took just minutes to reveal the answer once she arrived there.

'Pregnant!' she whispered as she stared in awful fascination at the proof. Without thinking about it her hand crept down to spread over the flat of her stomach.

How much longer would it be this flat? she wondered, all her training and knowledge suddenly deserting her now that *she* was in that position.

The sound of other voices snapped her out of her meandering thoughts and she pulled herself together, carefully disposing of the evidence lest other eyes should see it and guess.

I'll think about it later, she promised herself. Perhaps I can talk to Soph about it.

But she knew she wouldn't. This was a situation of her own making—albeit with a little help to supply the other half of the genetic material required—and she would make her own decisions about it. Then she would tell her sister what was going on and what she'd decided to do about it.

In spite of the fact that she was feeling definitely queasy, she was delighted to find that the department was frantically busy. What she needed today was to have no time at all to think.

Even so, it was amazing how often the thought of that tiny bundle of rapidly dividing cells came into her head, and no matter how often it happened, she still felt that same thrill of the first discovery.

It was going to cause problems in her life whatever she decided to do about it, and the prospect of making those irrevocable decisions was daunting, but somehow…

Somehow, the more she thought about it, the more she realised that, however it had come into being, she was absolutely bowled over by the thought that she was pregnant, awed by the fact that there was a baby growing deep inside her and terrified by the almost overwhelming responsibility.

Another realisation that took her by surprise was the subtle difference in her emotional response to her patients. For the first time she had something special in common with them and could truly empathise with their fears and concerns.

She hoped it was a good omen that, by the time she finished her shift, she'd brought another three perfectly healthy, perfectly normal babies into the world.

'Not that I want three babies,' she muttered with a shudder as she climbed into the taxi that would take her to her sister's house. 'One at a time is plenty.'

She settled back into the corner and realised that her hands had automatically come to rest protectively across her stomach. Suddenly, she knew that she didn't need any time to think about her decision. It had already been made from the moment she'd looked at the pregnancy kit and seen that the result was positive.

'Hey, little one,' she whispered as she pressed her hand against herself. 'This is your mummy speaking. I'm going to take good care of you while you're in there, growing, and I'll see you in about eight months.'

In the end she *had* confided in Sophia, and had been bowled over by her unstinting support.

It had actually been her sister's idea that she could go and stay at Granny Ruth's croft for a while—not that either of them could have foreseen that the "while" would stretch quite so long. Sophia certainly wouldn't have believed that anyone accustomed to city life could have settled so comfortably into such a simple existence, but to Ella it was just what she'd been looking for while she waited for her baby to be born.

She was still being very careful to give no hint to anyone else about the identity of the father of her child. With Sophia working at the hospital it wouldn't have been fair.

Anyway, she thought wryly, as the old expression went, it took two to tango. Seth couldn't have made her pregnant if she hadn't gone to bed with him.

The only thing she could fault him over was the fact he hadn't told her he was married.

Even then, honesty forced her to admit that she'd been so much in love with him that it probably wouldn't have made a difference to the outcome.

So much for her high-flown principles!

Still, her country idyll would probably be coming to an end soon. Once the baby arrived she was going to have to start thinking about earning her living again. Her grandmother's legacy wouldn't last long at this rate and she needed to keep some in reserve in case of emergencies.

She was already earning enough for a hand-to-mouth existence with her spinning and knitting. Would it be worth exploring other ways she could exploit those skills?

Perhaps she should think about investigating the possibilities of becoming a district nurse. That would mean she could stay up here and still have a job, albeit one with far more variety than pure midwifery.

There was still time to think about it, though. In spite of its increasing size, the baby wasn't due for another two or three weeks and she certainly didn't want to go back to full-time work for at least six weeks after that.

In the meantime, there were chickens to feed, eggs to collect and a storm front moving in with snow showers forecast overnight. Definitely a sign that she should stoke up the fire and draw the curtains against the world.

CHAPTER NINE

HOW could her idyllic life have been turned upside down and inside out in such a short time?

Just over an hour ago she'd been contemplating possible career changes and looking forward to an evening in front of the fire while the snow drifted down around her.

Thinking she was all alone in the croft at the head of the glen, she'd heard a sound at the door and had opened it to find Seth on the step, sent by one interfering older sister. Then, after a shouting match that had got neither of them anywhere, she had to burst into tears.

They hadn't lasted long, but could the situation get any worse? Ella wondered as she fumbled for her pocket in search of a tissue.

Silently Seth held out his hand with a perfectly ironed hankie.

Equally silently she accepted it and mopped her face then took a savage delight in blowing her nose, noisily.

The sharp ring of the kitchen timer was welcome, giving her an excuse to turn away from those far-too-intent eyes. There was some serious thought going on behind them if he was directing that first-class analytical brain to analysing her words.

The need to check on the bread baking in the oven also gave her a moment to gather her own thoughts and decide on a course of action.

It might have been a tactical error to tell him that he was the father of her child. What if his wife hadn't managed to have the child she wanted? Would Seth be legally entitled to claim her baby?

The thought was frightening, and if she'd had time to think perhaps she wouldn't have been quite so quick to hand him so much potential ammunition but…somehow it had been an automatic reaction to refute any idea that the child might have been fathered by any other man. How could it have been when she was still in love with Seth?

She turned towards him with a perfectly browned loaf in her mittened hands and lifted her chin, determined to be firm.

'Seth, I know Sophia sent you up here but I don't want you to stay. The croft isn't big enough and it…it isn't appropriate.'

He nodded slowly and for a moment she was sharply disappointed that he'd made no attempt to change her mind.

'I realise now how small the place is and how difficult that could make things, but if you look outside you'll see that there's no chance that your friend Malcolm would be able to fetch me. Ella, the snow's coming down faster than ever.'

'But—'

'And anyway,' he continued hotly, 'if you think I'm leaving now, when I've only just discovered that I'm about to become a father…' He paused briefly and closed his eyes, obviously reaching for his usual calm. 'Anyway, where could it be more appropriate for me to be than with the mother of my child? I take it that it's due some time in the next two or three weeks?'

'Give the man a prize for mental arithmetic,' she muttered sarcastically, hiding her uncertainty about his real reactions to her pregnancy.

'I'd rather you gave me a piece of that bread,' he returned blithely. 'Is there anything else to go with it? I'm starving.'

Her own stomach was feeling rather empty, in spite of the turmoil of the last few minutes, and she could hardly sit and eat in front of him.

'Home-made soup. Leek and potato,' she muttered ungraciously. 'Although why I should feed you…' She turned away to swing the pot across so that the flames from the fire began to lick at it, then lifted the lid to stir the contents.

A sound behind her had her looking over her shoulder to find that Seth had taken his coat off and found the soup bowls in the dresser.

Suddenly she could see just how much he'd changed since the last time she'd seen him.

In spite of a thick jumper it was painfully obvious that he'd lost weight, more weight than someone of his height and build could afford to lose.

His face looked almost gaunt and with glints of grey at his temples…

'Have you been ill?' she demanded abruptly, unable to help herself. She might be angry with the man for his duplicity but that didn't seem to stop her caring about him.

'Yes and no,' he said cryptically. 'Ill, as in have I had an illness, no, but…' He sighed deeply and shook his head. 'I'm sorry, Ella, but I'm just too exhausted to go into it yet. I need to eat and I need to sleep and then I need to come to terms with…' He gestured wordlessly towards the child she was carrying.

'After that,' he continued wearily, 'we need to sit down and talk about it.'

'I seem to have heard that line before,' she muttered as she turned back to stir the soup and pull the pot slightly to one side to prevent it burning. 'Cutlery is in the middle drawer.'

She recognised that there was no point in badgering Seth to talk any sooner than he was ready. She could see how exhausted he was. A good puff of wind would be able to rattle his ribs, as her grandmother used to say, and the only remedy she had available was good hearty food and a bed to sleep until he was ready to wake.

It only took another minute for her to cut several thick slices of bread and bring them to the table with a dish of locally churned butter and by then the soup was piping hot.

'Here,' she said as she ladled it into one bowl and then the other. 'Shall I put the kettle on for a cup of tea?'

There was a strange expression on his face when she turned round with a steaming bowl in each hand to find him looking at her in total fascination.

'What?' she demanded sharply, knowing that she definitely looked less than her best. Still, at eight and a half months pregnant and in a croft without central heating or double-glazing she was unlikely to be wearing anything more alluring than thick woolly jumpers.

'I was just thinking that this scene could be taking place at any time in the last couple of hundred years or so.' He gestured towards the simple cooking arrangements and the plain wooden table that had in all probability been made by one of her ancestors.

'I'm sorry it isn't anything more fancy,' she began, but he interrupted immediately.

'That wasn't what I meant at all.' He closed his eyes and shook his head and she was ashamed of giving in to her instinct to pick a fight with him. The poor man was so tired he could hardly think straight, let alone put his thoughts into words.

'So, what did you mean?' She set the bowls down on the table and gestured for him to take a seat.

She had to wait while he settled himself at the table and took his first spoonful of soup, pausing before he tasted it to inhale the enticing aromas of home-grown vegetables simmered in a rich creamy broth.

'Oh, yes,' he breathed with a look of bliss on his face. 'It tastes even better than it smells and it smells heavenly.'

He took another spoonful then paused just long enough to spread butter on the thick slice of fresh bread before he started eating again.

Eating? It was almost as if he inhaled the soup, it disappeared so fast.

'More?' she offered easily, already getting to her feet knowing that he wouldn't be refusing.

'Please.' He held out the bowl. 'Now, *that* is what I meant about the timelessness of this scene. There's no microwaved lobster thermidor or take-away curry, just a good honest soup that's probably been made to the same rule-of-thumb recipe right down the generations. The bread has just come out of the oven and the butter was probably churned by someone who's lived within a dozen miles of this croft all their lives. It's a simple nourishing meal and one just like it has probably been served for generations at the same table in the same spot. *And* it was probably served by women wearing hand-knitted jumpers and with thick woolly socks on their feet to keep out the winter chill. The whole scene is almost completely timeless.'

It was almost as if he already knew their family history and she certainly wouldn't be objecting to being compared to someone as hardworking and tenaciously independent as her grandmother.

'I'm glad you haven't got a hankering for take-away curry,' she teased, tacitly calling a truce. 'Even if it weren't snowing like there's no tomorrow, I think the nearest one is a forty-mile round trip.'

By the time he'd finished eating, the combination of sitting close to an open fire, a stomach full of hearty food and sheer exhaustion had him drooping where he sat.

'Seth?' she called the second time his head nodded and he brought it up with a jerk. 'Grab your wash kit and go to the bathroom while I sort out your bed. You need to sleep.'

Without a word he straightened up from the table and stumbled towards the bags still piled inside the front door, more than half-asleep already.

Ella's heart went out to him in spite of her determination to wait until he'd explained himself, and when he'd disappeared into the minor luxury of the modern bathroom she hurried into the bedroom.

The sheets had only been on the bed for one night so she wasn't going to bother changing them, but in the absence of central heating he would need them warmed up by a hot-water bottle. The other thing he would need, whether he normally wore them or not, was a pair of pyjamas, and somewhere in the back of the cupboard she was sure she'd seen a pair of her grandfather's… Ah! Here they were.

She carried her booty back into the living room, spreading the brushed cotton fabric over the back of two chairs by the fire to warm through while she boiled the kettle to fill the bottle and lit another lamp.

'Here,' she said when he emerged from the bathroom, offering him the bundle of warm striped fabric. Her heart warmed to him all over again as he stood there with a puzzled expression on his face, looking impossibly boyish with his hair sticking up damply in the front where he'd washed his face.

'What are these? They're not mine.'

'No. They were my grandfather's and unless you've brought some of your own, you're going to need them in that bedroom if you don't want to freeze.'

He gave her an old-fashioned look and turned towards the open door with the fabric tucked under his arm, moving unerringly towards the inviting warmth of the lamp beside the bed.

'Mind your feet when you get in. There's a hot water bottle in the bed.'

She watched him right up until he closed the door, the latch dropping into its rest with a sharp click before she turned back with a sigh to clear the remains of their meal away.

There were still several hours left until her usual bedtime, but somehow her contentment in spending those productive hours alone in the tranquillity of the croft had vanished when Seth had arrived. Now the cosy room just seemed empty and for the first time in a long time she felt lonely.

'So, have an early night,' she muttered crossly as she took the dishes and cutlery out to the sink in the scullery. 'Anyway, it's going to take you a little while to organise a bed for yourself.'

She hadn't told Seth that she was giving him her own bed, knowing that he would probably refuse it in spite of the fact that he was almost dropping in his tracks. There were two single beds up in the loft, the ones she and Sophia used to use when they came to stay, but it would be far too cold to sleep up there until she did something expensive with insulation.

For tonight, she would have to be content with bringing the bedding down and spreading it out in front of the fire. By the time she was ready to sleep it would be aired and she'd be as warm as toast.

Anyway, Seth would probably never know where she slept the night. She'd be awake long before him in the morning with plenty of time to fold the bedding away.

'What the *hell* are you doing there, woman?' roared an angry voice, dragging Ella out of the soundest night's sleep she'd had in months.

'What?' She lifted her head just enough to peer over the covers and found herself looking up and up a never-ending pair of stripy pyjamas.

The outraged expression on his face didn't have nearly the same effect on her as the fact that it was Seth's face at the top of those unbelievably ugly pyjamas.

She couldn't help it—she just roared with laughter.

Even stuffing a handful of blankets in her mouth didn't help, and neither did his affronted look.

'When you've quite finished, would you like to explain why a heavily pregnant woman is sleeping on the floor instead of in her own bed?' he demanded, tight-lipped. 'I take it that was your bed you put me in last night.'

She nodded, not chancing speech when she wasn't certain she'd got her mirth under control.

'Why, for heaven's sake?' He raked a frustrated hand through his hair as though tempted to pull it out.

'Because…' The urge to laugh had completely gone now. 'Because you were so tired you were nearly falling face first into your soup and it would have taken too long to get this bed ready.'

Her sincerity took the wind out of his sails but he glared at her for another second.

'Well, tonight you're going to be in your own bed. If anyone's going to sleep on the floor it'll be me.'

'Does that mean you're staying?' Her voice rose into a squeak and she started to heave herself up so that at least she was sitting. She felt at far too much of a disadvantage lying at his feet like a beached whale.

'Of course I'm staying,' he retorted, striding across to his bags to rummage for some clean clothing. 'Have you taken a look outside yet? It must have snowed all night.'

'So you can't leave.'

'Nor do I want to until we've finally got a few things sorted out and, knowing our luck, that could take weeks.'

As an exit line, it was a beauty, especially when it was punctuated with the latch of the bathroom door dropping with a sound like a gunshot.

'So,' Seth began again at the end of a largely silent breakfast, 'are there any chores that need doing outside? Any animals to feed?'

'Apart from the chickens, none that I need to tend,' she explained as she got up to collect their dishes. 'The family next door have been dropping hay for the sheep at the same time as they leave my milk.'

'And how far away is that? Walking distance, I hope.' He'd surprised her by following her through into the scullery as she began the washing-up, picking up a tea towel as though this was a chore they shared every day.

'Not when it snows like this. If there's any left at the drop-off point, the weather's cold enough to freeze it so it won't go bad. In the meantime, I'm well stocked up with dried milk so I won't go short.'

'So you've nothing to do except sit inside and stay warm,' he said with a satisfied nod.

'Except for my work,' she added as she drained the sink and reached for a towel to dry her hands, and he immediately frowned.

'You're not in any state to work,' he snapped. 'Even midwives get maternity leave.'

'Except I haven't been working as a midwife,' she threw over her shoulder as she went back into the living room to stoke the fire.

'I've been spinning wool shorn from local sheep. Some of it I sell, the rest I knit up and sell the garments.'

That revelation had silenced Seth completely and he watched, clearly intrigued as she positioned herself at the spinning wheel that her grandmother had first taught her to use when she was a child.

He was fascinated by the process, not least because she was able to use her hands and feet totally independently of each other to regulate both the speed of the wheel and the thickness of the strand of wool it was twisting.

'Is it hard to learn?' he asked after several minutes, obviously itching to have a go.

'Not if you can pat your head and rub your stomach at the same time,' she teased, then brought the wheel to a stop and relinquished her seat. 'Here. Have a go.'

It was the first time she'd ever seen Seth truly out of his depth, the neuromuscular skills that made him such an excellent surgeon apparently deserting him when it came to this ancient craft.

They spent several minutes absolutely helpless with laughter and it was a heart-warming sound that she'd never heard before.

The fact that he could genuinely laugh at himself when he was all fingers and thumbs and making a total mess could only endear him to Ella, as did his determination to master the skill.

It was nearly an hour later that he finally looked up at her with triumph written all over his face.

'It might not be pretty or perfectly even, but I did it!' he announced with all the pride of a little boy tying his own shoelaces for the first time, and Ella's heart squeezed.

If her child was a son, would he look like that when he mastered a new skill?

Something of her thoughts must have shown on her face because his own grew similarly serious.

'Ella, are you ready to talk, or at least to listen?' he asked huskily, his eyes the soft grey of polished pewter.

She sighed heavily.

She'd been dreading this ever since she'd realised its inevitability, but she still loved Seth too much not to hear him out. Anyway, they had to find some way to clear the air for the sake of the child they'd created, even if it wasn't the only one he'd fathered.

That thought had been the one that had tormented her most in the months since she'd moved here, so it had to be the first question he answered.

'Start off with your wife,' she prompted. 'Was the third attempt at IVF successful?'

Ella could see she'd shocked him.

'How did you know?' he demanded, clearly amazed. 'I never told anyone at the hospital anything about my private life so how do you know so much?'

'Sheer chance,' she said bluntly. 'One of our midwives doesn't like putting a book down without reading to the end. She worked with the two of you at one time and was hoping I knew whether the third session of IVF had been successful.'

His shoulders almost seemed to bow under an intolerable weight.

'No. It wasn't successful,' he said in a subdued voice. 'But she was so obsessed...' He shook his head then glanced up, briefly meeting her gaze. 'It's probably easier if I start at the beginning.'

Ella nodded then waited silently while he ordered his thoughts.

'Fran would have been a wonderful mother,' he finally said, the words so sad that they almost sounded like an epitaph.

'Almost as soon as we were married she wanted to start a family, but neither of us had finished training so we were sensible and waited a while. Then when we were ready and nothing happened we went the usual route and had tests.'

His hands were knotted together, hanging down between his knees as he leant forward with his elbows braced on his thighs, and his eyes were fixed intently on them.

'She was devastated when they told her that her Fallopian tubes were too badly scarred for her to become pregnant naturally. Apparently she'd picked up an infection some years earlier, water-skiing on an exotic holiday, and hadn't even known it. The water is forced up at such speed that the cervix can be broached.'

Seth flicked her a glance to see if she'd understood and she nodded.

He looked so lonely that she wished she dared to go to him to put her arms around him. Even though he might have been unfaithful to his wife when he'd slept with her that magical night, it didn't seem to stop her loving him and wanting to ease his pain.

'Then she started on the series of drugs to stimulate egg production and was absolutely over the moon when they were able to harvest nine eggs at the first try. She was so certain that everything was going to work that when the first implantation failed she was devastated.'

He rubbed his hands over his face almost as though he wished he could erase the memories but he doggedly continued.

'Even then, I was worried that the stress was too much for her, but she seemed to shrug it off and was raring to go as soon as she got the all-clear to start again.'

This time the pause was longer and his voice was wearier when he went on.

'It seemed to be successful the second time. For two months she was absolutely ecstatic, almost bouncing off the walls, and then she started to bleed.'

There was agony in his voice and she wondered if he'd ever admitted just how harrowing it had been for *him* to have to go through losing his potential children time after time. It wasn't only his wife who had been bereft and yet he'd probably been the one doing all the consoling.

'The specialist was adamant that he wouldn't let her try again for several months, to give her body and her mind a chance to recover. She was so angry and frustrated by the decision that she became absolutely impossible to live with. We were rowing all the time and it was tearing everything that was good about our marriage apart so I moved into hospital accommodation.

'It was just supposed to be a temporary arrangement, just until things calmed down, I told myself. But once we weren't living together I had to admit that I couldn't bear the thought of going back.'

He looked up, finally meeting Ella's eyes with a mute appeal in them. 'It's my fault, you see. If I'd been living at home where I should have been, I'd have seen what she was doing. She wouldn't have been able to get away with it.'

'Get away with what?' Ella's imagination was reaching overload. It was a wonder the man hadn't cracked under the strain long ago.

'She started the third attempt without telling me anything about it. Somehow she'd persuaded the consultant in charge of her case that she was physically and mentally ready to give it another try. She still had some frozen embryos from the first egg collection so she didn't need anything more from me, but because we weren't living together any more she wasn't certain whether I'd agree to fertilise any more eggs if the IVF didn't work this time. I didn't find out until later that she was so desperate that it should succeed that time that she was taking advantage of her position in the department to break all the rules. She managed to falsify her blood test results so that she could continue taking the drugs long after she should have stopped.'

The silence stretched out, the only sound in the room the intermittent crackle of the fire.

Finally she couldn't wait any longer.

'Seth, what happened? Did she lose the babies?'

'She never got as far as having them implanted. Apparently, she started having breathing problems one day at work, but before anyone could work out what was wrong she collapsed and went into a coma.'

'A blood clot,' Ella breathed, feeling sick.

It was one thing to be prepared to undergo all the numerous tests and procedures attendant on IVF and to undergo them time and time again, but she couldn't imagine being so obsessed with conceiving a child that she would deliberately risk her own life by flouting all the hospital safety measures.

'How bad was the damage?'

'PVS,' he said succinctly but there was a catch in his voice. 'Absolutely no chance of recovery but she lingered for months until finally she developed pneumonia.'

He looked up at her with a ravaged expression, his eyes nearly black.

'Do you want to hear the ultimate irony?' he demanded harshly. 'That phone call—the one I took during your sister's wedding reception—was to tell me that she'd just died and suddenly, after keeping the nightmare to myself for so long, I just wanted to tell you all about it.'

'But I persuaded you to dance with me and then, when we went up to the hotel room, I didn't let you talk.'

'That's what I meant about the ultimate irony,' he said heavily. 'The very day that Fran died as a result of her desperation to have a child was the day our child was conceived.'

Ella couldn't sleep.

For a start, she couldn't get comfortable enough, with that lump in the way, and turning over was almost impossible. Her back ached and the monster inside her hadn't been still for hours, in spite of all the books saying that babies grew quieter towards the end of a pregnancy as space become more restricted.

She'd actually been more comfortable on her makeshift bed last night, she thought with a scowl. This one was too soft for her to be able to move easily, but Seth had insisted that he wasn't taking her bed for a second night, even though the first time had been inadvertent.

She shuffled again then gave up with a huff of annoyance. It didn't really matter what she did, she wasn't going to be able to sleep, especially when she admitted that her insomnia was really due to all the thoughts tangled up inside her head.

She still felt close to tears when she thought about the hell Seth had gone through in the last couple of years.

It might have been some time since she'd last had any connection with patients undergoing infertility treatment but that didn't mean she'd forgotten the tremendous stress they could experience during the process. Even given the small number of couples she'd seen, she'd recognised the feelings of frustration, inadequacy and guilt. Then there had been the anger and resentment towards other successful couples, carefully camouflaged under smiles of congratulations.

Most destructive of all was the sudden plunge from hope to despair as yet another cycle failed to achieve their dearest wish.

It wasn't hard to see why such an explosive mixture could destroy a marriage, no matter how committed each of the partners were at the outset, sapping their confidence in their relationship and even in themselves.

What she didn't understand was her part in the tangle of Seth's life. Given the way she felt about him, she'd been stupidly relieved to find out that she hadn't been a party to adultery, but that still didn't explain all the other questions.

She sighed heavily and glanced at the old-fashioned luminous dial of her grandmother's alarm clock.

Nearly midnight. She'd been tossing and turning…or trying to turn…for over an hour now, and was no closer to sleep.

Was Seth sleeping? Would it wake him if she were to creep out and warm some milk, the way her grandmother would have done for her when she was a child?

She heaved herself out of bed and wrapped herself in her fuzzy old dressing-gown, rolling her eyes when she realised exactly how far apart the front edges were now.

Once upon a time they had wrapped over each other by a long way but even without the camouflage of oversized jumpers, she knew that her bump was growing huge.

She patted the hyperactive bulge with a wry grin before shuffling silently to the door in her thick warm bedsocks. Thank goodness she was going to be in a hospital with plenty of pain relief available when this elephant arrived!

She held her breath as the old iron latch gave its distinctive click then eased the door open as silently as ancient hinges would allow.

'Couldn't sleep?' Seth murmured, and she saw his shadowy outline silhouetted by the warm dull glow of the fire.

'I didn't want to wake you, but…I was going to make myself a drink.' She padded across towards the fire then detoured to collect a pan and some milk.

'Hot chocolate?' he asked, sounding artlessly hopeful, and in spite of the weight of her thoughts she had to chuckle.

'Hot chocolate it is.'

Once she'd given the fire a poke it didn't take long to heat the milk, and within minutes they were sitting with steaming mugs cradled between their hands, one on each side of the fire like bookends in their matching rocking chairs.

It was Seth who finally broke the silence.

'Are you having more broken nights as you get closer to the end?'

'Sometimes.'

Even by the light of the fire she could see that his eyes were on her, and when she glanced down she realised that he would be able to see clear evidence of the frantic activity going on inside her.

That brought home to her in a blinding flash the fact that it was the first time he would have seen his child moving, and she suddenly had to add guilt to all the other emotions roiling inside her.

The shock of thinking that she was pregnant by a married man had sent her scurrying for this convenient bolt-hole. The fact that so many people had seen her dancing with Seth, only for both of them to disappear from the room shortly afterwards, would have made conclusions only too easy to draw once her pregnancy had started to show.

Except that he hadn't been a married man but a recently bereaved one, and that brought her right back to her original worries.

She rested her head back against the chair and sighed. If she wanted to sleep, perhaps she needed to take her courage in both hands and ask the questions. She might not like the answers but at least she wouldn't be left wondering.

'Seth?' she murmured hesitantly, drawing him out of his own thoughts. 'I was thinking about what you told me and… Well…I wanted to know… Why did you sleep with me?' she ended baldly, suddenly opting for the direct route to what she needed to know.

He gave a bark of incredulous laughter. 'Why did I sleep with you? Why do you *think* I slept with you? After that night I would have thought it was obvious. Because I couldn't keep my hands off you any longer.'

Ella quivered as a sharp burst of awareness ripped through her. It was the same every time she thought of that night, but this time she wasn't going to let it derail her thoughts.

Before she could respond, he continued, 'Listen, Ella, I've always tried to be an honourable man, and even though Fran was in a coma, I was still legally a married man. In my book, that meant that it didn't matter how much I wanted you, you were out of bounds.'

It was good to know that he shared her principles about infidelity even though it could have been seen as a technicality in his situation.

'But why that night?' she persisted, finally coming to the crux of her fears. 'Was it some sort of…release after Fran's death or was it because you really wanted this?' She gestured towards her prominent bulge with a trembling hand, holding her breath while she waited for his reply.

CHAPTER TEN

'AND I thought you were a reasonably intelligent woman,' Seth said finally, when the silence had stretched out so long that Ella felt like screaming.

Suddenly he surged to his feet, making her gasp as he left his chair rocking wildly in his wake as he came to loom over her.

'If that was all I wanted,' he said softly, the two hands he planted on the arms of her chair trapping her as effectively as bars on a cage, 'would I have spent the last eight months eating my heart out, wondering where you were and why you'd left without a word?'

'But *you* left *me* without a word, the very next day,' she countered, glaring up at him furiously, barely registering the fact that she now knew why he'd lost so much weight. 'No one knew where you'd gone or why, or even if you were coming back. Once I discovered I was pregnant I didn't have any option but to leave, especially when I knew you were married. Too many people saw us dancing that night *not* to put two and two together and make four.'

He dropped his head and groaned softly before straightening up and backing off a pace.

'I should have spoken to you before I left but I knew what would happen if I woke you,' he admitted softly. 'I'd been working with you and watching you and learning as much as I could about you for months, but I was too afraid to tell you what was going on in case you didn't want to know. I couldn't risk it, not when you were the first ray of sunshine and warmth I'd had in my life for such a long time.'

'So where *did* you go?' Ella was calmer now, and filled with a rapidly growing sense of anticipation.

'First, there was the funeral, then there were all the legalities and all of Fran's belongings and the house to dispose of. It was still in our joint names but I knew I would never want to live there again. And then, when I'd done it all and drawn a line under the whole episode I was finally able to admit that I was completely exhausted and slept the clock round... several times. And in my arrogance, I just assumed you would be there, in the background, like some sleeping princess just waiting for me to turn up and claim you.'

Ella was honest enough to admit that, princess or not, if she hadn't been pregnant, she *would* have been waiting. If only he'd spoken to her, asked her to wait, they could both have been spared so much unhappiness.

Increasing discomfort broke into her thoughts and she held her hand out. 'Could you give me a hand, please?' she groaned. 'I don't feel very comfortable sitting too long these days.'

He took both hands and braced her, but as she straightened there was a sudden strange sensation deep inside and a swift gush of fluid.

'Seth!' she squeaked, looking down in disbelief at the puddle spreading around her feet.

'Oh, Lord,' he breathed. 'Not here. Not now.'

'I don't think we've got any option, unless you can come up with some bright ideas.'

'Where's the nearest hospital…? No. That's no use because we've no means of getting there. An ambulance. How do I get in contact with the nearest one?'

'Telephone, but there's no point trying,' she gasped, gripping his arms as she concentrated on breathing her way through an enormous contraction. 'Even if the lines are still up, they won't have anything that can get through that much snow.'

'What about the air ambulance? I could phone them on my mobile. They'd be able to make it up here.' He was sounding increasingly desperate while she was feeling unaccountably calmer with every minute.

'Specially equipped ones can go out in the pitch dark, but none of them can when it's snowing that hard.' She gestured towards the window he'd uncovered before he'd sat himself down to contemplate the flames half a lifetime ago.

It looked pitch black outside, without a single street light for miles, and it took a minute before the miniature drifts building up rapidly in the corner of each pane became obvious.

'Apart from anything else,' she added, 'the mobile phone companies' boasts about their coverage are wildly inaccurate. Very few people can get a signal up here unless they're sitting directly under one of those ugly masts.'

Seth exhaled heavily, the mixture of groan and growl perfectly demonstrating his frustration.

She drew in a breath of her own, feeling another contraction building already and knowing she didn't have much time.

'I know it brings the situation a little too close to two centuries ago for either of us,' she said quickly. 'But look at it this way. At least I get to have my baby delivered by my favourite consultant and you get to be the first one to see your child coming into the world.'

He groaned again but this time it was mixed with a measure of laughter until she leant against him with a deep groan of her own.

'Another contraction already?' Seth's tone had sharpened and she knew he had switched into consultant mode. 'How far apart?'

She shook her head. 'Your guess is as good as mine,' she panted. 'Wasn't looking at the clock.'

'Let's get you to the bedroom,' he suggested, wrapping his arms around her for support.

'I'd rather…dance,' she retorted, swaying gently from side to side as she focused on relaxing her muscles. It was definitely a lot harder now that she was actually doing it rather than just handing out all that glib advice, and she wouldn't have the benefit of any analgesics.

'I'll dance with you when this is over, but I need to have a look at you now.' He tried to guide Ella towards the bedroom but she dug in her sock-clad heels.

'Promise?'

'What?' His expression was totally confused.

'Promise me a dance,' she said insistently, although she couldn't have explained why it was suddenly so important.

Until she saw the way his expression softened, and then she knew.

'I promise you a dance,' he said with a gentle smile, then brushed her lips with a tender kiss. 'Preferably another Argentinian tango that will blister the paint off the walls.'

'I'm going to hold you to that,' she promised, just before giant hands seized her again and tried to rip her in two. 'Ow! That hurts!' she whimpered, and her knees refused to hold her up any longer.

'Ella, no! Don't do that!' he exclaimed, trying to support her weight long enough to get her into the other room, but it was hopeless. 'You're determined to do this as unconventionally as possible, aren't you?' he panted when he'd finally managed to get her settled on the makeshift bed in front of the fire.

'It's warmer here,' she murmured, desperately grateful for the few moments' respite from pain, but there was no time to waste, especially if her labour proceeded at this headlong pace.

'Seth, help me, please. I need to get some things together.' She held out her hand but he didn't take the hint.

'You don't need to do anything except lie there and practise all that controlled breathing you're always teaching the mums to do. I'll fetch whatever you need if you'll just tell me where to find it.'

It was frustrating, lying there shouting directions when it would have been so much faster to have found things herself, but even Ella had to admit that she was in no fit state to be wandering about the croft.

When Seth had helped her out of her wet clothes and performed his examination her contractions were already almost continuous, and by the time he'd assembled his makeshift delivery kit and a set of clothes each for mother and baby, she'd already passed through the ambiguities of transition and was ready to push.

Each pain seemed interminable but in an amazingly short time the head had been delivered and he was warning her to pant while he checked that the cord wasn't wrapped around the baby's neck.

'Ella, look,' he said in an awestruck voice, positioning the mirror so that she could catch a glimpse of their child. 'I can't tell in this light whether the hair is dark or auburn, but she's beautiful.'

'How do you know it's a girl?' she demanded just before she took another breath, the urge to push undeniable.

'If it's a boy, I'll apologise for calling him beautiful, but that doesn't mean I'm not thinking it,' he said, his hands gently and lovingly supporting the emerging child. He gazed up at her and held her eyes, his own gleaming suspiciously brightly in the lamplight.

'You're both more beautiful than I can tell you and I love you more than I can say,' he said softly, the words as powerful as a vow.

'You're going to have to work on your timing,' she grumbled, torn between elation at his words and the urgent need to push again.

There was a sudden explosive rush as the baby slithered out into his hands with an indignant squawk followed by a tremulous wail.

'I apologise,' Seth murmured before she could catch her breath, glancing from the child cradled in his hands to his mother. 'I shouldn't have called you beautiful.'

'It's a boy?' Ella breathed, tears of delight seeping into her hair as she gazed from one to the other. They were both equally precious to her.

'Are you going to feed him yourself?' Seth asked, his voice husky as he moved forward on his knees to place the child in the crook of her arm. 'Letting him suckle should help to expel the afterbirth.'

Something in his tone made her take a moment from admiring her precious son. Suddenly she realised how different childbirth was from the other side. Now that she was the patient, she was lying here perfectly content with the result of her labours. As the professional, Seth was still worried about the final stage of the delivery, especially as he had no means of summoning help if anything were to go wrong.

'I want to give feeding a try,' she said. It seemed crazy after the intimacy of what they'd just gone through that she should suddenly be shy when it came to something as relatively simple as setting the child to her breast. Except the last time that this had happened to her it had been Seth suckling her, and she knew from the way his eyes had darkened that he was thinking about it, too.

'He's quick on the uptake,' Seth murmured with a ridiculous amount of pride as his son latched on eagerly. 'There won't be much there yet, apart from colostrum, but the suckling will trigger the milk production.'

'Wow! It also triggers another contraction,' Ella complained, helpless to do anything other than grab for a hasty breath and push.

'Where did you have your scan done?' Seth asked a moment later, a strange tone in his voice. He'd waited until the pain had ebbed before he'd spoke again but Ella knew there was something he wasn't telling her.

'I never had a scan,' she said with an uncertain frown as she tried to read his expression. 'The day I was booked to have it there was a problem with the computer system, and as all my other signs and symptoms were perfectly normal I didn't bother booking another one. They were going to do it when I went into hospital to have the baby if they were worried about anything. Why do you ask?'

There was a brief cry of complaint as she switched the child to the other breast and then it was her turn to complain.

'Ouch! I've heard other mothers saying…that breast-feeding makes the uterus contract quite strongly…until it's returned to size…I hope the contractions…aren't going to be this painful for long,' she gasped. 'I might change my mind about bottles.'

'Oh, I don't think they'll continue for long,' Seth said with a definite chuckle in his voice. 'At least, not after the baby's been born.'

'But he's already been…' she'd begun when the penny finally dropped. 'Twins!' she yelped in a mixture of disbelief and delight, just before the next pain demanded her total attention.

This time things didn't move quite so smoothly or so quickly and she knew enough about Seth to see that he was worried.

'Tell me,' she said urgently. 'What's wrong?'

He paused for a fraction of a second with agony in his eyes before he spoke. 'She's a breech.'

'She?' Ella challenged again and was rewarded by a glimpse of a smile.

'This time I can tell the sex but not whether she's beautiful,' he said, then quickly put all joking aside. 'Ella, this is taking too long and there's a danger that the contractions could detach both placentas at any minute. We need to get her out as fast as possible.'

She gasped, understanding immediately just how dangerous the situation was for her baby. If her placenta did detach itself from the wall of the uterus it would be the end of the baby's blood supply, and with no blood supply she was going to run out of oxygen, fast.

The whole situation was frighteningly similar to one of the first cases she'd ever seen Seth operate on. That time, only the fact that he'd had a full complement of highly trained staff and all the resources of a modern hospital at hand had saved the mother and her child.

'Tell me what you want me to do,' she said steadily, knowing she was placing her life and that of their unborn daughter in his hands. She loved him and would have to trust him to do his best.

'She's a twin so she's smaller than she might otherwise be, and she's two or three weeks early. Also, the birth canal has already been opened by the first head, so the situation's not as bad as it could be.'

'But her head could still get caught like a cork in a bottle and I still need to use every second of every contraction…' she finished for him.

It hurt to see the look of despair in his eyes again, but she knew that he had already considered and discarded any idea of a Caesarean section to save the baby's life. They had absolutely no surgical equipment and the conditions couldn't have been less favourable.

'Contraction coming,' she gasped, drawing in a big breath and beginning to push, absolutely determined that her child wouldn't be lost through lack of effort on her part.

Over the next couple of minutes, every atom of concentration went into pushing harder and longer than ever. Seth was encouraging her every millimetre of the way, giving a running commentary as the legs were delivered and then the arms were freed one by one. Finally, in the dying seconds of the contraction, when Ella was so exhausted she didn't think she had any energy left, he ordered her to stop pushing.

'Pant, Ella. Pant,' he begged in a voice grown husky with unremitting tension.

She barely had the energy to do that much, peering out of half-closed eyes just in time to see him lift a tiny pair of feet up in the air as though teaching the baby to do a handstand. Clasped firmly between his fingers, he brought them towards her head while his other hand pressed almost brutally into the pit of her stomach as he tried to free the baby's head, stuck inside her like a cork in a bottle.

The indignant wail wasn't as vigorous as her brother's but it was definitely there and Ella closed her eyes on a swift prayer of thanksgiving.

'She's alive!' she heard Seth whisper in a choked voice. 'Oh, thank you, God, she's alive.'

There were tears gleaming on his cheeks as he tenderly passed her over and a trace of an exhausted smile.

'Let's see how much energy we've got between us to get those placentas out,' he joked tiredly as he gently persuaded the traumatised infant to accept the nipple. 'Come on, sweetheart. Try.'

'That's it,' Ella said, looking up at Seth as she felt the first tentative tug. 'Try again…for Daddy.'

She saw Seth blink, his expression priceless as the truth finally sank home.

'Ah, Ella, if you only knew…' He shook his head. 'I came up here under duress, a man who wouldn't admit how perilously close he was to some sort of breakdown, and within a matter hours you've completely changed my life.'

He drew in a shuddering breath as he fought for control and Ella took pity on him.

'You're very welcome,' she said softly. 'But I hope you remembered to move the lamp.'

'Move the lamp?' he glanced towards the one he'd placed on a stool near her feet so that it would throw as much light as possible on the pile of towels he was using as a delivery table.

'Well, these babies seem to be attracted to the light like moths and I think two is quite enough for this time.'

'Idiot,' he said with a chuckle and turned to check on progress.

This time the contractions weren't as strong but she could tell that Seth was worried right up until the second afterbirth was expelled.

It was there in his face as he straightened up and looked at her, the wide smile of relief that told her everything was well.

'Remind me, next time you're close to term, that you're not allowed anywhere where we can be snowbound.'

Ella grinned. 'Does that mean there's going to be a next time?'

Seth just looked smug as he took first one and then the other sleeping baby from her, wrapping each in a clean warm towel and placing them side by side in the old family cradle already polished and waiting for their arrival.

'That seems to be what happens when the two of us spend the night together,' he said as he scooped her up and carried her into the bathroom, seeming to know how much she wanted a warm wash. 'And I hope we're going to be spending many nights together from now on,' he continued when he finally deposited her in her clean nightdress in a bed warmed by a newly filled hot-water bottle.

'Seth?' Her heart was so full she wasn't certain she could find the words to tell him everything she was feeling. In the end it was easiest to concentrate on the most important fact. 'I love you,' she finished simply.

'I know.' He smiled and sat on the side of the bed to hold her hand. 'I knew when we shared that mistletoe kiss and it nearly broke my heart because I couldn't do anything about it, least of all tell you that I felt the same way.'

'Why *did* you learn to dance?' Ella asked, anticipation racing through every nerve as Seth led her out onto the floor and took her in his arms. 'It's unusual unless you come from a family that's mad keen on competitions, and I've been meaning to ask you ever since Sophia's wedding.'

'Blame that on my mother,' he said with a wicked grin. 'She was the dance enthusiast and she conned my brother and me into learning. She promised it was a good way to meet girls, then I found I enjoyed it.'

'And did you?' she demanded with a flash of her green eyes. 'Meet girls, I mean?'

'Only one special one,' he whispered as he drew her against his body and began to sway with her in time to the music.

It was the Christmas Ball again, and Seth was finally fulfilling his promise to dance with her. This time they wouldn't have to worry about wagging tongues if their dancing betrayed the way they felt about each other. The fact that as soon as the roads had been cleared of snow they'd taken a detour through Gretna Green on their way south had quickly become fodder for gossips and romantics alike.

Tonight they didn't have to worry about hurrying back to let the babysitter go home either. Sophia and David were babysitting the twins for the whole night and while it was the first time they'd been away from the children for a whole night, there was a suite waiting upstairs…

'Do you think David and Soph are coping with the two horrors?' Ella murmured, her thoughts running on similar lines. Ross and Ruth seemed to create far more than twice the havoc of any other almost-one-year-old, egging each other on shamelessly into one piece of mischief after another.

'If not, they need the practice. She's due in a couple of months,' he pointed out logically, then forced her concentration back on the dance with another series of complex blocks and steps then draped her seductively over his arm so that her breasts were just inches from his face.

'Seth!' she hissed, a tingling sensation warning her that her body was becoming visibly aroused by his tricks. Well, two could play at that game, she thought as she circled him, allowing the hand that trailed around his body in her wake to dip dangerously low. She gave in to the temptation to stroke the tight curve of his bottom but wasn't quite brazen enough to go any further—at least, in public.

Once they got up to their room it would be a different matter.

The rhythm of the dance took over, forging them into something that was infinitely more powerful, more responsive, more provocative than either of them was alone.

This time they were both smiling into each other's eyes when the music ended and they found themselves surrounded by an appreciative audience.

'This could become an annual institution,' Seth murmured as he swept her into a slow waltz and tried to edge surreptitiously towards the door.

'One of them,' she pointed out, knowing that his all-too-obvious arousal was only one of the reasons why they were leaving the dance.

'And the other one?' he prompted as they stepped into the lift and murmured greetings to the other couple sharing it.

'Wait and see.' Ella had to hide her smile, knowing that he'd been hoping the lift would be empty. Now he'd have to wait a couple of minutes before he began his seduction.

He tried to kiss her when they reached their door but she ducked to use the key-card as an excuse to stay out of reach. She didn't want him to pre-empt all her planning at the last moment.

'Come here, woman, and tell me what's going on,' he growled playfully, wrapping her in his arms as soon as the door closed behind them.

'Nothing's going on,' she said innocently, then glanced deliberately above their heads.

He couldn't resist following her gaze and she knew he'd understood the message in what he'd seen when that sexy smile crept across his face.

'You want another mistletoe kiss?' he asked in a husky voice.

'What sort?' she countered.

'I thought there *was* only one sort,' he said with a frown.

'No. There are definitely two. Both say "I love you", but only one comes with condoms.'

The love that shone in those pewter grey eyes would always make her heart take an extra beat.

'Shall we start with the kiss and see which way it takes us?' he suggested as he lifted her in his arms and took the single step that allowed him to brace her against the wall. 'With or without mistletoe, it seems to work just perfectly.'

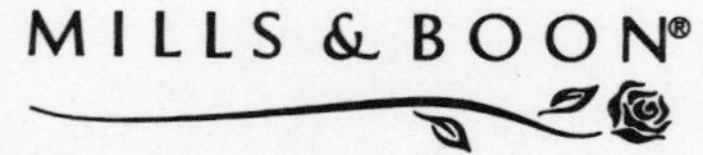